The Ballad

of

Buttery Cake Ass

Aug Stone

First printing: 2022
ISBN 979-8-218-09886-5

Cover art by Hanco Kolk
Cover design by Christine Navin

Other titles by Aug Stone:
Nick Cave's Bar
Off-License To Kill

SIP002

www.augstone.com

for Brian Ewing

ROBIN

ROCK N ROLL

Aug

INTRODUCTION - ROUND & ROUND

When we were like 15, 16, me and my best friend Trig used to go record shoppin'. And it was weird, our local record store had this counter, with all the cassettes behind it. The goods. You had to ask to see 'em. Music is a valuable commodity, I get it. Dudes sliding tapes into their baggy jeans, this was the mid-90's after all, even tryin' to swallow 'em to retrieve later. Ouch, right? The term 'heavy metal' doesn't do justice to that type of pain.

Trig was always after Buttery Cake Ass' *Live In Hungaria* album. Week after week we'd ask, only to week after week be disappointed. Truth be told, Trig much more so than I. I mean, I didn't know anything about Buttery Cake Ass. But that's the beauty of music, of any sort of artistic creation, that another's excitement for it can infect you like this. Though it seems Trig didn't really know anything about them either. And this quest for knowledge drove him, and us, to some rather strange places.

The thing about Buttery Cake Ass is that there's no actual record of them. I mean besides the fabled records that supposedly exist. No historical account, I guess is what I'm sayin'. I've no idea how Trig even heard of Buttery Cake Ass, but obtaining their *Live In Hungaria* became an obsession with him. A Holy Grail. And the whole thing was, it was called *Live In Hungaria* but no one was certain if it was a live album or not. I mean what if it was supposed to be pronounced *'live* in Hungaria' and it was like some spoken word advertisement by a faction of patriots who were trying to entice people to come to their Eastern European homeland? Turnin' folks on to Béla Tarr films so they can start readin' László Krasznahorkai novels all the time. You know what I'm talkin' about, I'm sure...

But me and Trig were travelin' far and wide lookin' for this record. And slowly, as those weeks rolled into months and, later, years, we started to put the pieces together. Not only was this album *not* by a prò-Magyar propaganda group, but it is doubtful that any member of Buttery Cake Ass ever set foot in Hungary, let alone recorded any music there. I mean this was the early 1980s, we were to find out, the Iron Curtain still firmly hanging and Iron Maiden just beginning their own quest for fire and 'World Piece'. I mean you hear about kids from West Germany sneaking under the metal drapery to East Berlin, Prague, Budapest and beyond to play secret illegal punk rock shows, but this would've been much harder to do from suburban America at the time. Especially when the band didn't even have enough money to leave their parents' garages. And yes, Iron Maiden did play in Hungary in 1984 as documented on their *Behind The Iron Curtain* home video, but that is neither here nor there. Well, it was filmed *there* and made available to watch *here*, thanks to the invention of the VCR, but you know what I mean. It has little impact on our story. By the time Iron Maiden were playing these concerts, Buttery Cake Ass had already recorded *Live In Hungaria*, and apparently it didn't sound anything like the New Wave Of British Heavy Metal. Though of course they loved Maiden, enthralled by their font and mascot Eddie as much as everything else.

Buttery Cake Ass' obscurity - the fact that the employees of Woodby's Music, our local shop, couldn't find a way to order anything by them, and the many radio stations we called, even the college ones that we listened to religiously, had also never heard of the band - only intrigued us further. After a while, our options dwindling, Trig had the notion to consult a psychic medium about the situation. He thought some of the members might have died, I don't know why. We went to a séance and nothin' happened. Not even any spectral jokesters claiming to have been the tea boy on the *Live In Hungaria* sessions. But this didn't deter Trig. We started driving out to graveyards all around, lookin' for any etchings on a tombstone that might read 'Here Lies (Blank), Loving Guitarist of Buttery Cake Ass'. But Trig soon realized that this was going to be awfully time-consumin'. From our small town in the States, this could take hours. And that's only gettin' thru one cemetery. Searchin' for any reference to Buttery Cake Ass.

One cemetery local to us, even. Which if they had hailed from our neck of the woods, well, you think we might have heard something about them somewhere. The trouble was we didn't know where they were from. And haphazardly - or even systematically - choosing burial grounds to scour would take longer than any amount of free time we had. Ya gotta remember that this was in the days before the internet, before we could just Ask Jeeves such a thing. But even with the web as it stands now, there are no records of the mighty Buttery Cake Ass. No Angelfire or Geocities tribute pages. Nothing.

Which is a shame, ya know?

And what if, like Mozart, the members of Buttery Cake Ass lay in an unmarked grave? That would be wild if it was in the very same cemetery in Vienna. Lending some credence to the much disputed 'Live' In Hungaria claims. The whole Hapsburg Empire, ya know? You ever have a slice of Austrian tort? It's delicious!

But this is assuming that anyone in Buttery Cake Ass had even passed on. Which for a band from the early 1980s is maybe 50/50 at best. So instead we decided it was easier to continue on to other record stores and talk to actual live people who might have heard - or at least heard of - this album. But as it turns out, finding a Buttery Cake Ass section at a record shop is as rare as seeing mention of them in a graveyard!

Eventually we were able - through the magical combination of sheer happenstance, dogged determination, and the kindness of strangers - to piece together a good part of the story, learning what few others have even opened their eyes to fathom. So grab a plate, pull up a chair, and treat yourself to the tale of one of the greatest bands ever unknown.

PART ONE - SWEEPING THE NATION

Apparently it all began when two young men by the names of Hans 'Floral' Nightingale, the *inestimable* Hans 'Floral' Nightingale in many people's opinion, and Hans 'Floral' Anderson both happened to start bands called The Floorists. With two O's. F-L-O-O-R-I-S-T, find out what it means to me, ya know? They even wrote 'em out with the quotation marks, though the word inside contained only the one O. Despite the band having two. I hope that isn't too obvious, and that I'm not wasting your time. I also hope I do not cause any offense to the two gentlemen aforementioned, but from here on out they will be referred to without the quotation marks, also aforementioned, as well as aforeseen, as after a while Trig and I stopped mimin' the air quotes whenever we spoke of them, their appellations seemin' to flow just as easily as Hans Floral Nightingale and Hans Floral Anderson. We've never met either party and again do not wish to insult them. If they preferred, we would of course speak to them usin' these gestures, performed with the utmost reverence. As you will see, I can imagine

Hans Floral Nightingale insistin' on this more than Hans Floral Anderson. But movin' forward, the quote marks, at least for these two luminaries, are implied. If you need a reminder, you can always come back to this paragraph. And if anyone representin' Buttery Cake Ass would like the text altered to include such punctuation, please do get in touch. Trig and I would love to speak to you regardin' many items of interest.

With that out of the way, let us resume our story. These young men were livin' at opposite ends of the same town. A community with no actual florist, make of that what you will. And they claim to have had the same idea independently of each other, which only adds to the strangeness of their relationship. Starting these bands before becoming aware of the other's existence. After which they argued for some time. Talkin' trash. Garbage that then had to be sent over to the other side of town to be heard. Traveling by word of mouth of course, I mean this was like 1979, 1980 at the latest. There was no internet back then, as I have previously pointed out. Trust me, the past hasn't changed in the time it took us to get to this part of the tale. Although one can only imagine how the Floorists chat rooms would've gone. Lawless places, full of, well, I shudder to think...

Finally the two Hanses agree to meet, to sort out this turf war in the realm of band names. Convening at a coffee shop on the outskirts of town called The Reality Café. And things got really real, just like you'd expect. Hans Floral Nightingale and Hans Floral Anderson each making the case that the moniker is rightfully theirs, presenting as evidence bulging notebooks in which they have sketched their respective Floorists logos hundreds of times. Bizarrely, these symbols look remarkably similar. An emphasis on the baseline of the drawings, the foundation as important as the name itself. Seeing an evolution from botanical patterns to a full-blown Dadaist approach to typography. Which more appropriately reflected each band's sound. Or at least the sound they spoke of wanting their group to have, for neither have written any songs yet. But their concept is strong - the floor, rock bottom but decorated with flowers. Each considering themselves the blossom that just might redeem the barrenness of their surroundings. The music would come later, they are confident of that. To be performed four on the floor, meaning, according to these two, as by a quartet with all their equipment on the ground. Four being the ideal number of band members that the Hanses have in their heads, picturing themselves standing on cement in a basement somewhere and making their way up, as they dreamt bigger and bigger, to the parquet tiles of a concert arena, sticking to their punk rock principles by keeping with the absence of a stage or drum riser. And over the course of their comparing notes and describing their eventual discographies, it dawns on the two young men that, maybe, they'd both had the same cosmic vision.

But what are they gonna do about it? Each has their own band already, two Floorists in a town with no flower shop. Though in truth, these groups were nothing more than each Hans and three other friends who said they might pick up an instrument one day. At the end of the evening - The Dark Night Of The Reality Café, the mystically-minded

12

might call it - after much rumination, difficult silences, and staring off into the angelic void, Hans and Hans each open their mouths to speak, and find they are about to suggest the same solution. They should both relinquish the name, that it is too precious, *sums up too much of our modern age*, to be trifled with. Too pure to fight over, to have any violence or animosity towards whatsoever, it's best just to let The Floorists go, to be swept off to the annals of history. Funny then how the band and its offspring have barely ever been spoken of or even acknowledged since.

Having returned home from The Reality Café, Hans Floral Anderson is left with blank pages of the calendar where theoretical rehearsals and band meetings would have taken place. Naturally neither outfit has ever played a show, and few outside the members themselves even realize these groups exist. His new circumstances bestowing upon Hans Floral Anderson all the time in the world to sit and wonder what to do with the rest of his life. After much soul-searching, he comes to understand that there is only one other musician in town, perhaps the world, who has the passion and ideas - the fortitude of soul - like he does. With such a revelation, Hans Floral Anderson promptly phones up Hans Floral Nightingale and proposes that - as the only two young men in the universe discerning enough to grasp the Floorist metaphor - they should work together. And an alliance that could have easily been fraught, turns out to be a most creative recipe.

Regarding the origins of the name Buttery Cake Ass, there's the rumor flyin' around, which many hold to be true, that it comes from Hans

Floral Nightingale in his capacity as something of an acrostaphiliac. Though some might say 'acrosticaddict'. Which is like it sounds, though I've heard it pronounced in different ways - *acrost*addict, acrosta*dict* - but whichever way the emphasis lies, the word obviously denotes someone who is addicted to acrostics. Acronyms, really. Though aren't acronyms acrostics in sheep's clothing? Some even say 'acro-addict' - *acrobatic* with letters, ya know? There are countless different terms for it, I'm surprised this isn't a more widely recognized condition in clinical psychology.

And with 'acrobatic', the prominent letters there are A B and C. The very beginnings. Also like 'abracadabra', though that brings D into it too. That magic word. And as the name of this band just suddenly appeared one day captivatin' Trig so, he was hopin' the records would spontaneously materialize too. I gotta tell ya I was worried for a while that Trig might be gettin' too into the acrostics game himself. Maybe not as an addict, but more than a recreational user. Writin' out stuff like The Record Is Galloping, The Route Is Growing, Time's River Illuminates Go-betweens...attempting to bring *Live In Hungaria* to him via supernatural incantatory means. You know, imitatin' your idols too much, like you do when you're a teenager. In this case a hero he had never seen nor heard before and knew almost nothing about. Maybe the most dangerous kind...

Though allegedly someone once asked Hans Floral Nightingale if the letters in Floorists or even Floral spelled out anything, and he gave them such a look that could only be described as 'world withering' and strode away off into the sunset. The heavenly orb conveniently doing so at the time, putting an end to the day and that particular line of questioning.

Hearin' this, I'd be hard-pressed to pose any further queries about the matter to him myself, but the rumor goes that they then had to figure out what to call their new band, The Floorists having been laid to rest with appropriate solemnity. And before they discover that Hans Floral Anderson has the voice they are after, someone suggests the duo ask their friend Becca to sing. And with Becca, Hans Floral Nightingale sees it as they are looking for both a singer and a name and, well, abracadabra, she has ABC and E! One step beyond, like that Madness song. As soon as he hears 'Becca', Hans immediately visualizes BCA, there being only one vowel for him. The first one alphabetically, of course. And truth be told, the E is a little too much for him to handle. You see how he was with acrostics, I'd hate to think of what he'd do with designer drugs. Of which I guess he would have to time travel into the future to obtain. Ecstasy may have around back then in certain quarters though it was all but mythical to the future Buttery Cake Ass. But still, Hans Floral Nightingale hears BCA and pronounces 'we can do somethin' with that'.

'How 'bout...how 'bout...Bringing...Carrots...Auspicious..ly?' Then after some consideration. 'Or no 'ly' maybe, let the adverb be implied.' Growing more excited with where his brain is taking him, 'Or like Beige Carrots Always...make a real statement!' I'm not sure why the C was Carrots so often, 'I C Carrots', like that Bruce Willis film, *The Crisp Sense* or whatever... But then Hans Floral Nightingale, knowing how quick this world is to persecute those of an artistic temperament, can hear the naysayers already, missing its poetry, and starting in with 'There ain't no such thing as beige carrots! You've done the farmin' all wrong if that's the case!' Stoically bearing in mind this criticism, though keeping with the theme, they forge on to Better Carrot Angles. Literally, that was the band name. Right from the get-go logo designs were proving problematic. Hans Floral Nightingale originally sketching the word 'Carrot' with its T representing the very thing. But when 'Better' comes along, the effect of having the two herbiferous letters right next to each other like that, with a third down the line, is disconcerting. Especially with its implications of a carrot tea. Not every supermarket carries that nowadays, back then it would have been pretty near unthinkable. The final draft becomes a mishmash of geometric shapes, before shifting to Berzerker Carrot Angels. Again, a likely inspiration for that same Bruce Willis film. And sure, the winged logo looks rad, but it is also the cause of many a sleepless night wracked with worry about the possibility of Aerosmith taking legal action, so they quickly move on to Babysitting Carrot Adventures, almost a decade ahead of its time there too. After tweaking this to Burning Carrots Alphabetically, although all still consider this to be a brilliant band name, they soon begin to have existential doubts, wondering if something else might better represent their collective creative force, other than this orange vegetable...

In hindsight, the feelings behind this switch are obvious from their use of 'Burning'. Scorched earth, spirit of '77, ya know? Pretty close to it too. As far as Trig and I could tell, this was around the tail end of 1980 now, early '81 at the latest.

When they finally do get away from carrots, which takes a matter of weeks, even months according to one source, they spend some time simply injecting the word Coconut into the pre-made carrot molds. Until they decide that this might be too much of a Monty Python reference. Though one might question just how much Bombastic Coconut Asemia bears any resemblance at all to anything Cleese & Co ever did.

It always seemed to be a given though that that middle C would represent a food stuff. As that letter is also the dominant key in the music of the Western world, the boys see this as a tradition they don't particularly want to break away from. Things really get cooking when Cookies are brought into the mix. Betelgeuse Cookie Astronomy, again pre-dating a major film here, is written with its A as a giant star, the O's exploding suns, and that K some sort of telescopic contraption, though it turns out all aren't so gung ho about this. Nevertheless, looking into space sees them leap forward in terms of the tunes they are writing. Though even these get swept away as they progress into Brushing Cookies Asunder, its H a broom, and then swapping that plural for a possessive to pull out of the magician's hat Besieging Cookie's Apartment.

The real life Cookie, Trig and I were later to find out, is quite the woman. Her warm and effusive soul shining through the imposing, stylish exterior that greeted us... But we'll get to that. Back around 1980, after attending the same high school as Hans Floral Anderson, Cookie did indeed have her own place where the Cake Asses, though still not known by that collective name just yet, used to hang out. Hours into our second conversation, she would tell us that the boys were too wrapped up in their visions of artistic glory to be much interested in romantic relationships, though she had a minor crush on both of them at separate times. 'Fleetingly injudicious,' she laughed, divulging that this was also true for most of the women in their friend group. She cast doubt on the notion that Hans Floral Nightingale was infatuated with Becca as might be implied by him using the letters of her name to inspire the whole BCA trip. Cookie putting this down to more of a quirk of the creative mind than any wildly misguided romantic gesture. She had not always been of that opinion, but we'll get to that too...

We asked her about the band name Besieging Cookie's Apartment, if it worried her at all that her home might really get taken over. Laughing, she told us that no, it was she herself who suggested it, not even aware of the whole BCA thing at the time, though in retrospect it's hard to miss. But that one day she said those words because the boys were always there, as she was their only friend with their own pad back then, and Hans Floral Nightingale wrote the phrase down immediately. Next thing she knew, she was being shown logo ideas and fielding questions about possible album titles. *Sudden Occupation Maps*, *Hidden Fortress Hair*, things like that... Finally saved by a telephone call from her father, Dr. Doone, who was quite a successful dentist in the area and the reason she could afford to have a place of her own at age 18. Casually mentioning that both Hanses were fascinated by the fact that it was her dad who was the one to nickname her Cookie when she was a little girl. Trig and I sharin' this sense of wonder. With him bein' a dentist and all, who amongst us wouldn't find this incomprehensible? Without ever meeting the man, Trig and I have conjectured about this for ages now.

There is a period of eleven days where the group happily rehearsed under the name Besieging Cookies Assumption, which they felt dealt quite thoroughly with their feelings towards that last band epithet, taken as it was from a literal supposition of Cookie's. This is also notable for being the only known instance where they use the same word starting with B twice in a row across two different monikers. Dropping the possessive apostrophe with this new one, thinking this lent the title an air of the mysterious that young men are so desperate to have at that age. The Hanses considering that maybe changing up the name like this might bring them one step closer to moving into a place of their own together, still living as they are in their respective parents' basements and practicing out in Hans Floral Anderson's mother's garage. A letter from Hans to Cookie, written the first time he ever fully felt the effects of marijuana, listing its contents as 'filled with sometimes a lawnmower, not sure where it goes when it isn't, an assortment of rakes of millions of colours - orange, green, the other ones, I think tan, all shades of brown actually, I'm not currently in the garage so I'm doing all this from memory. An old bike that I haven't ridden in years, one very lonely roller skate, its other half forever lost, an old EZ Bake Oven box, three-quarters-empty paint and gasoline cans, and other vessels containing who knows what! A deflated basketball poetically laying near a broom - a hefty broom I might add - and a crushed grape soda can that no one can ever be bothered to pick up'.

Besieging Cookies Assumption seemed there to stay until a real life incident prompts then bassist Dave Up to suggest Hans Floral's mother's solo project, in light of the snack she had only minutes before brought out to the practice space, could be called Burning Cookies Authority, provoking a great rift within the band. The cookies were charred, there is no doubt about that, but Dave tries to cover his tracks when he sees how mad Hans Floral Nightingale gets in defense of his friend, saying that no, he was talking about freeing themselves *and* Hans' mother from the bonds of any sort of baking goods. Of course no one is having any of this, Dave Up up and leaving before it gets really ugly.

When Hans has sufficiently calmed down and auditions have found them a replacement bass player, Bright Chili Autumn is proposed as the new name, to wash away the bad taste of the last. Hans Floral Nightingale, whose brainchild this is, assuring the others that by Chili he means the delicious Mexican stew, but that he won't argue if anyone wants to interpret it seasonally. After all, he likes the seasoning in most bowls of chili. And thus the logo designs morph to reflect this multiplicity of meaning, striking a delicate balance between the opposing sensations of sipping a spicy mélange in the brisk air of an

October twilight, surrounded by the magnificence of its foliage. No one knows why this one doesn't stick, it very much suiting their sound, as well as the cool brightness of a lot of the good music from back then. Though of course there are conjectures that maybe they gazed into the future and saw ablaze there another acronym, that of TLC, and knew this could get confusing, planning as they are to be in it for the long haul. This supposition of clairvoyance is found wanting though, as such hypothesis doesn't take into account viewing their own trials and tribulations, at which they surely would have bristled. For by time TLC were declaring themselves Ain't 2 Proud 2 Beg in 1992, BCA might've found the temptation too great to do the same with regards to making their record available, as *Live In Hungaria* is nowhere to be found. One could argue that you can't see what it isn't there, and the album, especially with respect to record shop shelves, most definitely is not. Nevertheless, there seems to be some sort of occult phenomena associated with Buttery Cake Ass. At least according to Trig. Hence the séance...

All are delighted when a group effort spawns Borscht Chowder Anomaly. The O in each word fashioned into a line of uniform soup bowls, causing even more excitement. That is until an older cousin of new bassist Davey Down scolds them that it is too critical of the two-party system, and that rock bands have a tough enough time trying to make it as it is without any government hassle thrown in, what with Reagan crackin' down on Thomas Pynchon like that... This confuses everyone in the soon-to-be-formerly Borscht Chowder Anomaly. Especially as their tunes aren't political in any way. Hans Floral

Anderson wondering what Davey Down's cousin might hear in them. But not enough to ask.

Another double meaning that suits their story - at least to those of us who can be counted as recipients of the legend - is Brilliant Capers Anonymous. Its middle S somersaulting over the subsequent A in perfect conjunction with the spy film font. This one has a lot of legs until it is revealed that some bandmates are bigger fans of those salty little buds than others. Once this critical info is brought to light they have no choice but to change it. Cookie jokingly suggesting Brilliant Cookie Anonymous but Hans Floral Nightingale shoots her a much put-upon look, punctuating it with the comment 'but we know who you are', before turning back to flipping through the cookbook in his hands for more ideas. After this exchange, Cookie always sensed Hans thought she was trying to worm her way into the band. Which couldn't have been further from the truth, as she didn't much care for their sound.

They are soon on their way to another appellation. It's strange that one of the only established facts about an otherwise completely obscure ensemble is that, at this point in their career, all four members of the band *quite liked chard*. Their predilection for the leafy green known above almost anything else about them. Plus they referred to it as chard and not 'Swiss chard', another odd bit of lore to survive the sands of time, though helping to alleviate the later problems we would face with *Live In Hungaria*. But they relished it enough, for a while at least, to call themselves Better Chard Act. Drummer Max Beta even, temporarily, amending his surname to Beta Vulgaris, in honor of the scientific species term for the vegetable. I remember asking Cookie the question that was on everyone's minds, certainly mine and Trig's - Were there *other* chard acts they were competing with at the time? Cookie just shot me one of those withering glances of the kind Hans Floral Nightingale used so effectively, and I shelved the query for good.

Everything seemed hunky dory in the land of Better Chard Act. Up until another existential crisis disclosed to them that their sound wasn't *heavy enough* to warrant such a band name. And nor, they realized, did they particularly want it to be.

Bear in mind, they still haven't played any gigs yet.

But as existential crises usually are, this was a useful revelation. And enough time has passed since the cookies debacle to make a return to that sort of flavour desirable. As spring approaches, so too does a sense of fun, a lightness of being - not to center us too much in Eastern Europe, especially now we had definitively found out they were a tried and true American band - and soon they are ready to play their first ever show. Pumped to take the stage as Bowling Candy Aardvarks, evoking the pure sugar rush of all great pop music that is one of their many stylistic sensibilities. On the night, there are only a handful of people in attendance, and the main trouble is that this handful's hands are busy occupying themselves with large polyurethane orbs, the gig taking place at, you guessed it, a bowling alley. And thus a good percentage of the crowd believe they are simply called Candy Aardvarks. When Hans Floral Nightingale hears this, he goes ballistic. *Bowling ball-istic*. Max Beta and Davey Down wrestling him to the ground before he can reach one of the conveyor belts, intent as he is on tossing said spheres into the apathetically misinformed crowd and doing countless dollars worth of damage and bodily harm. Such action is justifiable to Hans, to whom it is so obvious that this name would need a word starting with B to kick things off and make the hallowed BCA. And they were practically spoonfeeding it to these unappreciative ignoramuses by appearing at a venue where the letter is so prominently on display. Both 'bowling' and 'ball', and for that matter 'both', as well as 'beer' at the 'bar', all beginning with B. The be all and end all. Without it, the whole thing falls apart.

It is around this time that the Hanses write Because, Cinnamon Answers. With a comma after the 'Because', as that's the word she uses to reply. Apparently a lovely tune, combining the minimalism of Wire with how Hans Floral Anderson recalled his soda pop tasting the first time he saw *Star Wars*, and incorporating a rhythmic mnemonic device Hans Floral Nightingale had for remembering the moons of Jupiter based on the poetry of Baudelaire, somehow giving the tune the lush 60s love theme they were going for. Though you might've surmised all that after I told you about the comma. Unfortunately, they had abandoned this song by the time they finally settle on Buttery Cake Ass, feeling that the two phrases just don't mesh. Hans Floral Anderson emphatic that the cake in question is not only *not* cinnamon, it is also un-fla-vour-ab-le. That even if he did have a taste in mind, he would never reveal it, wishing to leave those possibilities open for the listener.

There is, allegedly, a cover of this song on a 7" single by Question Reveal Parrot, the BCA reference undeniable in the way those first initials are arranged. Though nobody knows anything about them either.

Cookie was unsure if a real life Cinnamon existed. She didn't think it was her. Though the inner workings of songs can reveal the strangest things...

But, before the danger of audience supposition sets in, they become rather taken with this particular flavour. And soon Better Cinnamon Abacus is bursting at the seams. Almost literally, because if you play the beads of an abacus like a musical instrument, and if they're made of, well, any spice or powder really, naturally they're going to burst. This was probably the closest the Hanses ever got name-wise to the worldview they had with The Floorists. It's clear that Better Cinnamon Abacus summed up something essential about the human condition for them. How life is ostensibly about trying to make a better computational machine, despite its lush aromatic counters crumbling by their very nature. All this at a time when processing power could still be regarded as in its infancy.

Nevertheless they do play a few gigs under this moniker. But when they tally those in attendance - on their fingers most likely, probably not on an actual abacus, even in the early 80s abacuses - abaci? - whatever the plural is, were largely a thing of the past. Though the band members could have been mentally picturing an abacus as they counted on their fingers, I wouldn't rule that out. Once the numbers have been totaled, however, they reconsider. Maybe another change is necessary...

And at this point, what name can they possibly go with?

Max Beta suggests BC Abbreviation, but this is deemed too religious by the Hanses.

Winter is soon rolling around again and it is tempting to go back to Bright Chili Autumn. Especially as they're consuming vast amounts of the stuff at the time, being one of the cheapest options at the grocery store. Davey Down once living for three weeks off four cans of generic Medium Spice With Beans and a package of expired hot dog buns.

But like I was saying about the weather, this necessitates some serious lip balm. NOT Serious Lip Balm the pop group, obviously theirs is more of a summer sound. But serious lip balm the real deal. And who doesn't love the taste of cherry? That was the mainstay back then. It's not like now where you have more lip balm flavours than there are words in existence, what with your Pineapple Goat Cheese Zinfandels and all the Umami Coffee Apple Strudel Seltzers... And Peach, of course. Buttery Cake Ass woulda had a field day naming their band if they had formed in this new, no-holds-barred, millennium.

But in 1981, cherry was all we had. The boys appreciating that, when taken together, The Runaways and their song Cherry Bomb offer a fine display of letters. Not that the Cake Ass ever sounded anything like any glam rock coming out of LA, or anywhere else for that matter. Though such is the power and scope of that fruit, that the Hanses & co. have trouble wrangling it into something meaningful to their own music. Boiling Cherry Afterthought was probably the closest they ever got. Perhaps if it had come to mind earlier... It must be said, though, they really did have a knack of hitting the nail on the head sometimes with the way their band names reflected their feelings about their *earlier* band names. And despite possessing a Budding Cherry Aesthetic, they never actually used that phrase. Even with how apropos it was to so much of the sound of the early 1980s.

Again it would be the cookie that leads them on to the next phase of their C, reinforced by the fact that it is Becca who delivers the inspirational treats to rehearsal one night. The Hanses are pretty strict about not having outsiders at practice but then again anyone bringing them food is surely welcome. Money to eat is hard to come by with how much work they are putting into the band. And Becca is special for being the one who had set them in motion, although it seems Hans Floral Nightingale has long forgotten this. Probably for the best, Becca muses as she watches him scarf down said cookies as if he's never even heard the phrase 'table manners' before. But baked into those very treats is a nut that is still some decades away from receiving its proper due. You may have deduced that I'm referring to the delicious cashew.

Becca leaving the plate behind to go get ready for her date that night. But Cookie, having accompanied her to Hans' mother's garage, stays with the band and said plate. And it is here that she tells Hans Floral Nightingale that perhaps this isn't the best way to go about winning Becca's heart. Using language that Hans will forever after associate with the yummy new taste of the cashew nut, his face turning cherry red at Cookie's implications, flushed with an amalgamation of a thousand unnameable emotions.

Hans proceeds to kick up quite the storm, no letting withering looks suffice this night. Stomping around, screaming and, occasionally, when feelings go well beyond words, pausing to pick up his guitar and strum a B minor 7 flat 9 chord, voiced BAC, the order of the notes he believes to be properly expressing his rage. How could Cookie accuse him of such tomfoolery? Of course he isn't sweet on Becca! If you like a lady you certainly don't go about impressing her by christening your new beat combo Bridal Cream Agency or Backseat Curry Agility in her honor. Though here again he pauses, pondering this last appellation. Being as it includes yet another double meaning of the victual involved. 'Curry', he repeats, before discarding the idea and resuming his rant.

Cookie really felt for Hans. He was undoubtedly embarrassed - one sensation that could be called out - and most likely covering up some real feelings for Becca. Those off-the-cuff aliases he threw out were rather risqué. And with 'bridal' too, that was serious. But there are also the colossal pressures that have been brewing at rehearsals. the consideration that maybe with this constant turnover of band names, along with all four of them never really being able to get unanimously behind a logo, they don't actually know who they are, even after so long, and they just want to get on with it, find themselves and conquer the world. At least with The Floorists they felt they had a ready-made mission statement and both Hanses yearn to get back to that earlier, more primal, energy.

Which of course leads to Bitter Cashew Advice. The whole band rallying around Hans Floral Nightingale, temporarily agreeing to the epithet to show their support for, well, whatever was going on with him.

Cookie leaves the garage after Hans grows quiet, but waits a few minutes outside, telling us that when they finally did pick up their instruments, she had never heard them play so well. Provoking a change in her feelings towards the group's music, for a little while at least.

After much reflection though, Hans Floral Anderson, Davey Down, and Max Beta all realize they aren't resentful people. Hans Floral Nightingale doesn't suspect himself to be either, even if his manner often presents itself otherwise. It becoming clear that Bitter Cashew Advice isn't the image anyone wants to project. Such words would be better relegated to a song title, and even then it would be best to just banish this incident altogether from their collective memories. What they are really after is something more playful.

Which one day, after talking about how great it would be to install a snack machine in their practice space - one you obviously didn't have to pay for - and then trying to work out how they can get it continuously stocked by the candy bar companies without having to purchase such replenishments either, or at least on the cheap, maybe a sponsorship deal or somehow getting the goods wholesale... well, in the midst of all this rhapsodizing, Hans Floral Anderson is bending down to change a 9 volt battery in his flanger pedal and glancing over, notices the EZ Bake Oven box, sitting there half-forgotten-like in the corner. Prompting him to suggest, 'How about Battery Custard Arcade?'

Custard really being the dream to have in any machine of this kind, a fantasy they've often reveled in on their way to go play Pac-Man or Space Invaders at the local video game emporium. Hans Floral Nightingale suggesting that maybe there could be another little battery-powered apparatus inside that actually cooks the custard once you press the button. Work begins straight away on a logo that turns the rounded areas of the As, Es, U, and Ds into miniature Suns whose light would heat up the dessert. As with so many of these names, Battery Custard Arcade belies the fact that they don't really understand how most food is made.

And then there is the night when it all comes together. Bitter Cashew Advice and Battery Custard Arcade having been hot on the heels of each other, some friends, and even band members, could be heard using them interchangeably. Picking up momentum to cross-pollinate and produce Battery Cashew Arcade and Bitter Custard Atlas, not that these should be confused with functioning entities in any way. Cookie says that in the immense excitement no one could remember who it was that, in the end, spoke the fateful words, long time coming as they were. Naturally later on everybody laid claim to doing so. Each having the feeling it was the next logical step, sitting patiently on the tip of everyone's tongues. Buttery Cake Ass. What they have been waiting for these long hard months of struggle, suddenly makes its way past someone's lips and all present are shocked into attention, recognizing its arrival. Approval flying around the room. 'Yeah man, this is the nazz... The now... The stuff that legends are made of...' Little did they know how right they were.

And so they're off. As Buttery Cake Ass. A gift of divine inspiration they're gonna run with. Get the butter churnin'. Metaphorically, of course. After so much trial and error they've learned that any notions of cooking should be in name only. Their part is proclaiming the ingredients. All the rest, the meal that is in a state of becoming, would, presumably, be served later. That's not to say that they didn't spend some serious time in the early days brooding over whether or not to have someone actually churning butter on stage. And maybe even vegan butter, as the rumors about the group's dietary habits often point to. Which makes the band name all the more punk rock. Even going so far as to rehearse a cover of Bob Marley's Stir It Up complete with churning gear before abandoning the whole scheme as cost-prohibitive. Not that Buttery Cake Ass ever sounded anything like The Wailers.

Cookie quite rightly conjecturing to Trig & I that if it was nowadays, someone would take your pre-order as you walked into the venue and you could pick up the vegan butter after the gig. But back then, these were guys who were continually trying to scrape up enough money to get an apartment of their own. They couldn't imagine having the bank balance to start any artisanal merchandising operations.

But storms pass only to return again later. I never understood if this wasn't the doing of that nursery rhyme 'rain rain go away, come again some other day'. I mean if you don't want it there in the first place, why would you tell it to come back at all? And who has ever engaged in meaningful conversation with precipitation? I know plants need watering, especially if they're gonna make that vegan butter. And what would the likes of Tones On Tail, The Cult, and, speaking of EZ Bake Ovens, Eurythmics do for song titles without rain? All those other artists too. Obviously Buttery Cake Ass, despite not sounding anything like the above acts, still would've needed to water those initial carrots to grow to where they are now. Though where they are now... You can't leave a cake out in the rain. Oh man, that's the saddest thought.

But they do have a period of elation with the new name, a sense of everything coming together. For a few days at least. Before the prolonged discussion about incorporating live churning leads to whether or not this will necessitate adding a fifth member. It being rather difficult to both churn and play guitar at the same time. I don't think Jimi Hendrix even tried. A major hurdle being their insistence on the classic four person line-up. Most of their favourite bands are quartets and ever since they had found their *nom de guerre*, Hans Floral Nightingale has become taken with the fact that they are four of them, denoting a square, while a cake is round. He considers this an augury that they will never be pigeonholed, citing the old saying about boxy pegs and circular orifices, and therefore given the freedom to create whatever they like. And with the music they would go on to record, in a sense, he was right. But not in a way that would have pleased them, or any artist for that matter.

Max Beta, being the drummer and used to having to carry the most equipment, wisely points out that even if it was empty, a full scale churning vessel would be pretty hefty and take up a lot of room in the car. An ongoing concern as Max is the only one with a vehicle, a second-hand Datsun Cherry that has enough trouble as it is transporting the entire band, let alone the gear. They were always having to rope some other automobile-owning acquaintance in with the promise of a free ticket and some drinks to join the convoy hauling their stuff to gigs. So again in his capacity as the drummer and thinking this new instrument would fall into his domain, Max suggests they bring back the mic'd abacus. As a tribute to their earlier name and a nod to the whole Cake Ass/Floorists philosophy, instituting a cool light show that gives the *illusion* of cinnamon beads breaking and the dust hovering around the abacus and its manipulator before descending in soft clouds to the ground. But then of course Hans Floral Anderson being the singer, feels the suggestion is aimed at him and he starts speculating aloud 'Do I stop playing and just... abaci while I sing?' Everyone wondering if you can use 'abaci' both ways like that, as a plural and a verb. Or if it is even a word to use at all?

Hans Floral Nightingale arguing that this would still require hiring another member, auxiliary percussionist or not, because - and he makes a fair point - if you're going to have such a cool device on stage, you want to give it the spotlight it deserves. It can't just be one part of a repertoire, a notch on somebody's bedpost. Even if that bedpost is used to churn vegan butter. Eventually a compromise is reached, but only after Hans Floral Nightingale has wrestled with his conscience for a considerable amount of time. In the end, the sacred square of the ensemble winning out over the single line of a sole instrument's, if you could call it that, exaltation.

It comes down to a chance encounter with an old school friend, one Byron Thebes. Believed by the band to be an 'electronics whizz', though Byron himself feels he has a lot more to learn before he would dare use this knowledge to apply for any professional position. Byron is back in his hometown grabbing a bite to eat when he spies his old schoolmate Hans Floral Anderson coming through the diner's doors with the rest of the Cake Ass after rehearsal. Calling them over and the five grabbing a booth together. Hans Floral Nightingale wasting no time in releasing his inner chaos concerning the use of an abacus versus the band member count onto the newcomer. Byron listening attentively as Max Beta picks up the threads, explaining the matter in more practical terms. The next evening turning up at Hans Floral Anderson's mother's garage with an abacus hooked up to a series of foot switches and a small lighting rig he has been messing around with. Instinctively placing these near Max's drums but then standing back to realize how the set-up blocks the beads. Hans Floral Anderson moving them in front of the floor tom within easy reach of his own area of operation. Launching into Gekyll & Seek, letting long chords ring out while Hans Floral Nightingale plays his usual lead lines, giving himself space to flick the beads in time with the lights. Both under his control, it seems to work. The abacus is highlighted tastefully, and also in such a way so as to not have anyone suspect the flavour of the beads which would then lead to assumptions about the cake. It feels right too to have one of them play it, someone whose songs these are rather than merely a hired gun abacus artist. Thus keeping them to the idealized four piece. However, Byron Thebes becomes so vital to their evolutionary next step that he is sometimes referred to as 'The Fifth Buttery Cake Ass', much to the chagrin of Hans Floral Nightingale.

Hans is, however, much relieved to have the member number settled so they can concentrate on other essential matters such as the logo for this long sought after name. Hans Floral Anderson much of the same mind, bringing into rehearsal the very next day a notebook half-filled with ideas, considering the cream of the crop to be the one having two lightning bolt S's at the end of the final Ass. The others skeptical, knowing they can't use it, being of course too close to KISS, but shocked that Hans Floral Anderson hasn't noticed this himself. Hans explaining that along with showing the band's dynamic fire, the electricity would be cooking the cake as well, his brain still seeming stuck on the word 'batter'. Growing pains perhaps, or maybe simply muscle memory from having sketched such an emblem countless times throughout interminable schooldays. When Davey Down brings up the resemblance, Hans Floral Anderson says he can't see it, especially as his S's are perfectly parallel whereas KISS' are not.

The culinary arts have a hard time escaping capture within Buttery Cake Ass' visual representation. For even Hans Floral Nightingale's initial layouts show the two T's as electronic hand mixers, with the U originally a bowl before progressing to an oven. The others excuse Hans Floral Anderson as each have looked to their own record collections for inspiration, all hoping one day to see a concert poster proclaiming a sold-out world tour where the Rolling Stones' mouth is eating a design that reads 'Buttery Cake Ass'. Not that they ever sounded much like a band that might open for the Stones. Umlauts are flirted with, again their little circles seen as some kind of Suns heating up the mixture à la Battery Custard Arcade. It is Hans Floral Nightingale who starts to move the band on from their earlier concepts when he nixes the umlauts but keeps their idea of roundness. The absence of an O makes it difficult to truly portray a cake or other aspects of their name, but being so literal isn't necessarily what they are after. For indeed when it comes to music, another body part dominates. Sure, you have to shake it on the dancefloor, not that Buttery Cake Ass' music was conventionally danceable, even with that notion in the early 80s becoming more fluid as new styles were exploding across the world's sound systems, but even so, you have to hear music first. It enters not through your ass but via your ears. Hans quickly sketches a simple arrangement with its central C expanded by two concentric half-circles to look like one such organ. The effect is disconcerting, especially to anyone outside the group, but, eager to move on, Hans Floral Anderson, Davey Down, and Max all accept it. The symbol even puts Hans Floral Anderson in mind of that quote about music being the food of love, conveniently forgetting its ending regarding the destruction of appetite. Instead leaving Hans wondering if Shakespeare would have used the KISS S's for the two in his name if he had lived in the 70s.

With new name and logo finalized, and their first gig with these now only weeks away, little do the mighty Buttery Cake Ass realize what is in store for them as they prepare for glory.

PART TWO - ICING THE BODY ELECTRIC

'Trig, we've been up for 3 days', I remember exclaimin' at one point. And we had. Trig says he got the idea from a high school math teacher regardin' how to best study for exams, but I'm not sure he got that right. Trig was claimin' that once the hallucinations kicked in, they'd give us valuable information about where we could find the records we were after. The treasure that would be revealed to us as our reward for concentratin' on them so hard for three days straight. I'd like to say I didn't have the heart to tell him, but it was more than that. I hadn't been fully focused on Buttery Cake Ass these past 72 hours. I mean, I was a bit. But certainly not at Trig's intensity level. And I admit I was a bit scared to confess this to him, especially in his sleep-deprived state. Who knows what he might do? And if his attention was so fixated, was my own mental power strictly necessary for this to work? Had I blown the whole thing? There was the harrowin' possibility that he might make us start at the beginning, and do it all over again.

I mean luckily we weren't drivin' anywhere during this time. I'm almost ashamed to admit what we *were* doing. But in the spirit of full disclosure, we were camped out on a hill across the street from Desert Island Discs. With a pair of binoculars and a couple bags of nacho chips despite Trig's steadfast belief that this was surely the record store where we would find what we were lookin' for. That there was another S implied in the 'Desert' of the shop's name. Me arguin' that if this was the case, why didn't we bring some Fruit Roll-Ups or Hostess Cupcakes to snack on?

Quibbles like this aside, we were just alternatin' shifts watchin' the place. Making sure there were no deliveries of any Buttery Cake Ass albums. Which seems insane, right? Cause they were long out of print.

But someone could be gettin' rid of theirs, was Trig's logic. I tried to point out to him that anyone bringing in a pile of vinyl to sell, well, we'd only be able to see the top one. It's not like we had x-ray vision. But I brought this up around hour 20 and Trig assured me that a secret section of our brains was about to kick in and soon enough we'd be able to sense the records, feel them in our bones, even the ones we'd never heard, or heard of, before. I tell ya at one point I got so excited when I thought I detected a bootleg cassette of Eric Dolphy playing with The Partridge Family in someone's pocket. But when I grabbed the night vision goggles, it turned out to be just a pack of cigarettes. I mean I shoulda known, Dolphy had died six years before the show even aired. And I guess I'm glad it wasn't some television exec trickery...

I tell ya though, when we finished that vigil, I slept the sleep of the just. Thirteen hours straight. Dreams soundtracked by the sweetness of Little Eva's Sugar Plum. But Trig had no such luck. Our venture had not metamorphosized into a metaphorical Night Before Christmas. And I think the fact that we hadn't found a copy of *Live In Hungaria* under any, again symbolic or even real, pine or fir trees in the area, or even a plausible lead for one, really hung heavy on his soul. He was awake for another 12 hours, just tossin' and turnin', like that Bobby Lewis song that Peter Criss later covered. Or if we're gonna stay with the Little Eva analogy, it'd totally be Locomotion. If we wanna extend that to the Kylie Minogue connection, Spinning Around too.

Man, it took us forever to find out about Desert Island Discs in the first place. The owner baffled by Trig's sleep-deprived ramblings that his shop was missing an S. Finally, once he realized that we weren't gonna buy anything, I think just to get us out of there, he did agree that yes, his store would've been the perfect place to find an album by a band called Buttery Cake Ass.

Though maybe I shouldn't completely discount Trig's methods. Later that week, no doubt set in motion by the challenges he had constructed for his body clock, Trig had a dream that there was a record store 47 miles North West of Desert Island Discs, as the crow flies. Or most birds, I would guess. So come the weekend we set out for it first thing. After askin' five different, though similarly confused, groups of citizens on the street, we learned there wasn't a single record store in that town. Trig would later link this to the lack of florists where the Hanses hailed from, but at the time we weren't privy to such enlightenin' information. We just seemed lost. But it was a nice sunny day and we had the windows open and tunes cranked up, and half an hour and a handful of towns later we're passing a shop with 12"s in the windows and a sign that reads GOOSE TRAIN. Trig swingin' the wheel back in its general direction.

When we walked in, what was bizarre was that it sounded like Eric Dolphy playin' with Magazine! Which is so much cooler, ya know? And man, I tell ya, it was like Trig knew. I'm not sure if it was the music or just this huge sense of the right time and place, but watchin' Trig and the owner of this shop, witnessin' their dance - figuratively of course, I've never seen anyone dance in a record store...which is kinda odd when you think about it, considerin' the surroundings... - but their graceful movements around the topic of Buttery Cake Ass was a thing of beauty to observe. The way Trig's face lit up when the owner - Fred, we were to find out his name was, on our first try too - replied in the affirmative to his question. Despite the ultimately despairing nature of his words, it was still like catching a glimpse of one's destiny in the mirror. I couldn't help but be affected by it. Though I really wish the Samantha Fox picture disc on display hadn't distracted my eye at pretty much the same exact second as Trig and Fred were experiencin' that initial soulful connection, somewhat tarnishin' the moment for me.

I grabbed a Brian Eno record to cover it up. *Taking Tiger Mountain...*, hoping the fox and the tiger would get along. That was my strategy. And then I looked at the Eno section again and by movin' *Tiger Mountain* I had uncovered *Before And After Science* and that kinda set me straight. These were vinyl records, not a literal tiger and fox, and approached from this scientific point of view, I had nothin' to worry about. The two would-be hunters would not be gettin' into a scrape in the middle of these unfamiliar environs keepin' me from hearin' the conversation and takin' in this beautiful encounter as I mentioned before. Safe in this knowledge, I turned my attention back to Fred's reply.

It must be said, he was excited too. I think we all had goosebumps. Maybe this was constantly happenin' there and that was why he called the shop Goose Train. As if you're tied to the tracks but ready for what's about to hit you, lookin' forward to it even, the great anticipation... Now 'anticipation', that's a weird word. It's got 'anti' in there but then like what's 'cipation'? Did they mean 'citation' like in Good Vibrations? So it's like something that stands perfectly still? Or is it part of the *precipitation* family? A warring faction within? Ya know, because it's anti-. And as I've pointed out before, you can't have a conversation with rain. Same for snow and all the other ones too. The postman's creed, ya know? It's easy to posit yourself against something that will not answer you back. So I guess we might never definitively learn if they're related or not. Or does 'anticipation' simply mean nice weather? But then you might be anticipatin' a storm, you know what worry warts we all are. Is this why birds fly south for the winter? 'Goose Train' was certainly apt.

So Fred's all 'Buttery Cake Ass? It's been a long time since I've heard that name. I'm still searchin' for *Live In Hungaria*. Used to have their first single though...which might even be rarer...'

Trig's eyes were bulgin'. Like goose eggs. Right there in the sockets. He'd had no idea. I didn't either, in case you need me to clarify. It's not like I had this incredibly valuable information about an early Buttery Cake Ass release and was holdin' out on my best friend. I mean, why would I do that? For one thing, I coulda gotten a lot more sleep!

But then Fred started tellin' his story and those eggs in Trig's eyes just cracked. The yolk of sorrow, ya know... Fred recallin' the time, three years previous, that his entire 7" collection - literally thousands of records, and that's a lot of inches, 14,000, if we take the plural of thousand as two thousand, likely even more than that, and probably not such a nice round number either - was stolen. Trig and I on the edge of our seats. Even though we were standin' up. Like dancin', there aren't many chairs in record stores as a general rule. And there weren't any in this one. Except for Fred's stool, of course. Which I wouldn't count as a seat open to the public. And anyway Fred was standin' too, what with the strong emotion runnin' through the three of us as he related what was in those 7" boxes. The Hillel Slovak & Keith Levene split with Kendra Smith doing that German lullaby, *Sarapoly* - the Sarah Records board game housed in a single sleeve, the Postcard Records first pressing of The Go-Betweens' *I Need Two Heads*, Gol Gappas' *West 14*, a plethora of early Wire singles...

...and Buttery Cake Ass! Trig was practically cryin'. Big goose-egg yolky tears brimming to flow down his face.

The story gets even more wild. Fred hired a private eye, as any sane man would, and the bounty was eventually recovered from a huge cargo crate hidden under a bridge in a small West Coast port. No relation to the Red Hot Chili Peppers. But yes, *read*y itself to be shipped out to destinations unknown. I'm sure you'll appreciate the Missing Persons reference, because otherwise he might have had to call his shop Missing Records. And that doesn't give a customer confidence. But it was appropriate to the situation we were now in. Because when he did get his collection back, it was all there. Except for the Buttery Cake Ass *Formaldehyde Hydro!* 7".

Cookie told us that after they settled on the name Buttery Cake Ass the air became electric around her apartment. The band continuing to spend a great deal of time there, as the Hanses still hadn't made a move to finding their own place. And the tune Formaldehyde Hydro was a product of all that excitement. An attempt to capture the spirit of what they sought to achieve. It was a matter of some debate whether or not to include an exclamation point at the end - well, obviously at the end - or if the phrase Formaldehyde Hydro was energetic enough, compromising with the title of the 7" containing the bold punctuative symbol but the actual song itself going without.

Cookie explaining that they felt using 'formaldehyde' in the title of their very first mission statement would make it clear that it was more than just about cake, even something you *wouldn't* wanna put in your body.

And they become convinced that spelling the accompanying track with a G - although F H G isn't *quite* the same order as B C A - points to its intangible profundity. Never in a million years did they foresee people pronouncing the b-side with a hard G to make it *Gek*yll & Seek. The G needs to be there, this is self-evident, and the band naturally assumes everyone will speak the G-E-K-Y-L-L spelling as 'Jekyll', like the precedent set with the famous literary character. They also argue that most anything starting with G-E - gesture, germinate, geothermal - obviously gives it that crazy J sound.

But when they hear people calling it 'Ghekyll', well, Hans Floral Nightingale especially goes off the rails. Shrieking and screeching about how they are tarnishing the sacred by not paying attention to the basic rules of pronunciation. How then could he rely on them to truly appreciate Buttery Cake Ass' artistic genius? And heaven help those who would dare pronounce it 'gheen-ee-us'!

Cookie put it best when she said 'I mean, gee whiz....' And that's kinda all she hadda say. But she went on, not really needing to clarify after that 'gee whiz' that she of course pronounced Gekyll & Seek in the correct manner, but informing us that those on the 'ghekyll' side then tried to cover it up, cowardly pretending that Hans had heard them wrong. And when that didn't work, Cookie told us they were all prostrating themselves before Hans Floral Nightingale, because by now there were some hangers on, enamored by the sounds coming out of the garage, as often happens in small towns where something like this might be the only thing going on. These mushmouths then switching tack, trying to make Hans Floral see the brilliance of their mishearing. That it is supposed to be like a gecko, who could change colours à la a chameleon, and despite being unheralded by Herbie Hancock, that that's how they'd hide... So with 'seek', it's a twist, cause geckos also camo up in a predatory way. And not like dressing as Arnold Schwarzenegger for Halloween, he wasn't so much of a household name back then. It would still be a few years yet before he was well-known enough for Twisted Sister to dedicate their *Stay Hungry* album to him.

Hans Floral Nightingale listens to their apologies but he can't make heads nor tails of how they'd miss that formaldehyde points to embalming. The hydro of course negating all the bad luck associated with death like that, which again takes it back to the Floorists' philosophy, this time with fake funeral flowers. The energy of the whole title moving a lot faster than a dead lizard *ever* could. And even though the chastised claim to see the point now, nodding their heads in agreement, Hans Floral Nightingale again grows irate screaming that 'an embalmed gecko doesn't change colors!' It's this phrase, apparently, that is etched in the run-out groove of *Live In Hungaria*.

I say 'people calling it ghekyll', but only 100 copies were pressed, and far less sold at the time. Though I hate to think that the term 'people' might be too much of a plural.

Cookie thinks some of the records might have even been destroyed. And there was talk of bringing them to sacred musical spaces and leaving them as an offering - throwing one off the Tallahatchie Bridge, burying a copy in Rockaway Beach... I had to drag Trig back into his seat when he heard this and luckily Cookie assured us that she didn't think it ever happened. Trig set to go diggin' up the oceanfront and drain the river. Though speakin' of rivers, Fred told us he got it straight from the source. The horse's mouth. I guess if the horse is drinkin' at the mouth of a river...do I even need a metaphor here? Fred was driving cross-country and, unbeknownst to him, ends up near the Cake Ass' hometown. Being the obsessive he is, as at every point on this journey, Fred pops into the local music emporium. A place called Graph City Records.

Not only is the stock of the highest calibre, there is also a fridge full of soda pop at the back next to a pinball machine. Fred is stoked, marveling at what a rad set-up this is. Wonderin' why all record shops don't feature such items. Opportunities to not only learn about, listen to, and buy great music, but also hang out even longer with refreshments on hand, and even to set the old silver ball game in motion. So of course he has to give it a whirl. And Fred said it was the darnedest thing, kismet really, that when he goes to put his quarter into the slot he drops it. Then notices the bottom of the pinball machine is covered in black velvet - curtains if you please - and feels the irresistible urge to part them and peer inside. What he sees there is astounding. Crates of 7"s, and in the very first one facing him, a sleeve that reads *Buttery Cake Ass - Formaldehyde Hydro!*

Without even thinking he might be doing something wrong, Fred grabs a copy - in his mind he remembers there being nine or ten in the crate - and brings it up to the counter. The man behind which happens to be the owner, Walter, who eyes him with a look of surprise, before sighing at Fred's query of 'What is this?', and lapsing into calm. Fred could tell that Walter was a gentle soul, an inkling that will flow into a final draft as Walter begins to regale him - for Fred did indeed feel regaled - with his story.

Beginning with how these kids would come into his store almost every day after school, riding their bikes down. And that he always worried about them getting that vinyl home. Especially one of them - and here he presumably meant Hans Floral Nightingale - who seems like he wasn't above ridin' dangerously, poppin' wheelies into traffic and whatnot. Stuff you really shouldn't be doin' if you got a bag full of records on your handlebars. But they'd be comin' in, showin' him the band logos they'd spent all day sketchin' on their brown-paper-bag-covered schoolbooks. He could tell they were artists and had a lot of ambition and ideas, which reminded Walter of his own teenage years. Bringing Kinks, Velvet Underground, and Stooges albums to class to trade with his friends. The day senior year of high school that Silv brought in Funkadelic's newly released *Free Your Mind...And Your*

48

Ass Will Follow was perhaps the most excited he's ever been in his life. Rushing to the nurse's office before second period, faking a cough and mystery ache to get sent home and put the alluring platter on the turntable. It working its magic. The record, especially the opening title track, is one of the wildest, grooviest, awesomest things he's ever heard, even to this day. Of necessity, he learns patience. He wasn't gonna get away with something like this every time. So he'd carry the records with him, throughout the entire morning, music being too holy to hide away in a locker, and learning in math class that album sleeves are perfect to draw the axes of a graph with. Immersing himself in the psych and art rock scenes of the early decade, by 1974 Walter has freed his mind enough to think it's a good idea to open a record shop. By then he has learned other uses for album covers, but when searching for a name he recalled those halcyon days of tradin' tunes in the hallways with Silv, Eight Ball, and Johnny No Thumbs between classes. Settling on Graph City Records, a tribute to that glorious time of falling in love with music and its infinite possibilities. When in late '76 he manages to obtain an import copy of AC/DC's Australian-only *T.N.T.* album, their cover of Chuck Berry's School Days reinforces to him that he is doing the right thing. So he was delighted to see kids comin' in who are carrying on the tradition. Wondering if they too spent time choosing the right album sleeve to use for each particular homework assignment.

It even seems that they had formed a band together called The Floorists. Which Walter thinks is clever because there is no flower shop in town. Hans Floral Anderson and Hans Floral Nightingale apparently showing Walter their differing Floorists designs within hours of each other and he just assuming it's the same group, why wouldn't you? That in the democratic process of deciding on a logo, everyone was trying to come up with the coolest-looking lettering they possibly could. Neither Fred nor Walter had any idea of how deep those Floorists tensions ran. And so Walter watched unawares as the hostilities were set aside and the new band develops, the two Hanses starting to come in together to shop and chat about records. At one point even hanging a handwritten sign in the window for a new bass player. Walter getting to see most if not all of the 25 different iterations of the BCA theme before they finally settled on Buttery Cake Ass. In the meantime, having a few side hustles going himself, taking over the empty shop next door and connecting it to sell both records and a wide assortment of archery equipment. Saying the link between the two is obvious. The perfect bull's eye of placing your favourite album on the spindle. He'd even sell records for people to use for shooting practice. Upstarts who claim they can thwack it right in the center hole without damaging the vinyl. Never parting with any of the good stuff for this of course, that would be sacrilege. Often heard to comment how 'ginchy' coloured vinyl would be with concentric circles of yellow, red, blue, and black, just like a target. Even getting some used books in, on music and archery, and trying to import some of the zines from the bigger cities, again about both topics. Both as in each, I guess. I can't recall a single zine that ever featured the two together in the same issue.

People start coming from around the state to check out his wares, with Walter making a little bit more dough as a result. And as any music bug in the early '80s was prone to do, Walter secretly desires to try his hand at a record label. He's driving miles to go see bands in some of the bigger towns nearby with an eye to offering them a deal, but soon the Cake Asses bring him in a cassette. And he is blown away by what he hears. As a statement of intent, which all debut 7" singles should be, this has a power and uniqueness that he knew needed to be committed to vinyl. Plus he's had a long association with the Hanses. They'd certainly spent enough money over the years to fund a small pressing.

Unlike the Cake Ass, Walter was quick in deciding to call the label Graph City Records after his shop, and even writing up a press release reiterating the schoolwork connection. Unfortunately, in more recent times, long after all the initial hoopla, a local periodical would find this sheet of paper left unread in an office drawer and decide to retroactively run the story. A spotlight piece appears, 'ReDISCovered', making no mention of Buttery Cake Ass or the label, choosing instead to quote his thoughts on academia, which has the unforeseen effect of regional conservative groups adopting Walter and his store as a model for how music should reflect and encourage study. A model in name only, for parents soon find out Walter's stock is anything but the 'wholesome music' they are expecting. Still, once the seed has taken root it finds itself growing amidst a battleground. Suits begin daily excursions to sweettalk Walter into stocking more 'Sounds Of The Righteous', or buying up The Exploited's *Dogs Of War* or Iron Maiden's *Women In Uniform* just to get them off the shelves.

Though he could never have foreseen such extremes, even back at the beginning Walter knew that life is not without conflict. The slab of vinyl must be penetrated by the needle for us to experience its beauty. So after spending a couple days with the Buttery Cake Ass tape on repeat, he thinks 'Why not, let's press up 100 copies and hope for the best...'

Trig was all chompin' at the bit now, askin' Fred for directions to Graph City Records. Again, in those days there were no online maps. It was someone writin' routes out for you by hand, with, if you were lucky, a sketch of the roadways that might make some semblance of sense.

Fred puttin' out calming hands in front of him, lightly pressing them towards the ground, indicatin' for Trig to take it easy, and lookin' for all the world like if David Bowie went from the photo shoot for the cover of his *"Heroes"* album to go referee a high school basketball game. I guess in Germany, I do not know. Were there organized youth basketball teams in Berlin in the 70s? If he had to fly to America to do so...well, I'm not sure how that fits in with the whole groundbreakin' collaboration with Eno, his metaphorical point guard, but it would have to somehow. Maybe even his metaphysical point guard, for who can really comprehend all the ways the astral plane presents itself here on Earth?

Readin' the situation - the *sitch* - better than my overexcited friend, I said 'woooooooooah, Trig...Fred's obviously got more to tell us *about*

Buttery Cake Ass. And besides, this was more than five years ago,' - not to bring it back to Bowie and his bball conundrum - 'who knows if Walter still has those copies?'

Trig settled down, but I could tell he was jonesin' to get a move on, torn between findin' the records themselves and soakin' up all the information he could about the mysterious group.

Fred continued. Tellin' us how he snapped up that 7" quickfast, along with ten or twelve other enticing discs, mentioning to Walter that he'd never even heard of Buttery Cake Ass, that they weren't in either edition of the *Trouser Press Record Guide*.

Walter replying with a sigh. 'Well you probably wouldn't have, would you? It's been about six years and I've still got that many left. Whole other box of them under the one you were flipping through. I don't even put 'em out on the shelves anymore in case these evangelicals try to destroy them.' At this point he briefly puts his head in his hands, muttering 'here come some more now'. And sure enough the door opens to three aging men desperately trying to appear hip. Walter having just enough time to tell Fred under his breath that he believes the rock t-shirts they're wearing are fake. That those bands espousing these ideas of innocence and orthodoxy as emblazoned on both sides of their garb, complete with logos, were nevertheless made-up. I mean who would do such a thing?! Perusing his catalogues, Walter could find no way of ordering anything by acts like Pure Ray or the more metal-looking Crossbow. Even if they pronounced it Cross*bough*...

And so Fred was off, a bit spooked by the disruptors of this otherwise excellent store, last seen peering over the Punk New Arrivals section. He wishes Walter well, thanking him and hoping he will see him again soon. Fred getting back in his car, totally stoked to go listen to his new purchases, as excited as he imagined Walter was when he was faking to that high school nurse with a Funkadelic album up his sleeve. It being 5 o'clock in the evening, well past the time any school nurse would still be on shift, Fred simply cruises on for another six hours as is his wont. Stopping for a bite to eat and, when the street signs begin to seem like they are written in Cyrillic script, pulling into a cheap motel for the night. But tired as his eyes are, his very soul is too amped up now, thinking about those goodies in the seat next to him the whole way. He could barely concentrate on any of the tapes he'd made for the ride. So when he gets to his room, Fred decides to drag in his stereo equipment, nestled tightly into his trunk so no one would think of stealing it, and setting it up, cranks the volume to throw on *Formaldehyde Hydro!* first thing. It's like an express train to heaven. And hovering now within these spheres of elation, Fred blasts the record repeatedly long past midnight, until the cops finally come to shut him down. Throwing his headphones on, and knowing he won't be able to go a whole 'nother day without hearing it, grabs a blank cassette. He's been meaning to make a tape of his purchases along the way, but then reconsiders and just fills all 90 minutes with the same two Buttery Cake Ass songs. Good thinkin', by the time you're done with one, you're gonna wanna hear the other again. And with rewinding, aside from the extra time involved, there was always the danger of the player eatin' the cassette, especially so in those days.

Fred being a man who has been dreaming of opening his own record store, sometime during the eternal hour of 3 AM, realizes what he has to do. Phoning the front desk for a wake-up call of 8, to get on the road and head straight back to Graph City. A six-hour drive in reverse. Four times that 90 minute tape straight through. But this is his mission, laid out before him. When he arrives, shivering with a sense of destiny, ready to buy up all the remaining Buttery Cake Ass stock, he strolls up to the door, practically walking on air, only to be greeted with a sign reading 'GONE SHOOTIN''.

Fred said his heart stopped for what felt like an eternity. Steeling himself, he peers past the window blinds to an inside much changed. The place looks empty. Of course he toys with the idea of breaking in, the records he wants are hidden below the pinball machine, but he can't even see that from his vantage point outside the glass. Had the evangelicals purchased everything in one go? For some unholy bonfire, or worse? Or had Walter just had enough? Packed it all up and skedaddled? Fred spends another couple days in town, trying to figure out what has happened. But no one he speaks to has any idea, and he eventually has to get to where he is goin'.

The whole experience is so painful, that Fred even forgets the name Graph City for a while. When it comes time to open his own record store he keeps tryin' to recall it for a tribute. The word 'Rhapsody' routinely appearing in his mind, though he is sure Walter's shop started with a G. Reminiscent too of that other Australian-only AC/DC release, Crabsody in Blue. Although he knows this isn't it, the double

R of Rhapsody Records puts him in mind of railroads, the animals soon crossing species, and leading him on to Goose Train.

Cookie also was at a loss to explain what happened to the shop, though her face lit up at the memory, exclaiming 'I remember Walter!' Telling us how cool the place was, that she'd found the Dolly Mixture *Baby It's You* 7" there. But she moved away long before Graph City closed, eager to experience more of what life has to offer. She had had enough of everyone coming to her house, wanting instead to explore the other bed and living rooms of the world - the more exotic the better - taking her copy of *Formaldehyde* with her to use as a coaster like she'd always intended. For it did look cool, she informed us. Although Graph City Records' first setback had come quickly when Walter's valiant efforts to manufacture a record using the classic archery colour scheme within the vinyl itself proved beyond the bounds of the pressing plant's capabilities, what they did come up with for its sleeve was enough to catch the eye of any seasoned record shopper. Art direction also having the unintended benefit of scaling back the Buttery Cake Ass logo which, since its inception, has grown quite out of hand. Hans Floral Nightingale continuing to tinker with his design and, by the time of the latest show flyer, he has added so many parallel and concentric squiggles that each letter is now three lines deep. There was no way to contain such elaborateness within the borders of the 7" square, thus necessitating a getting back-to-basics and removing all extraneous strokes. The cover itself more neon than formaldehyde, featuring the three primary shades of, not archery, but light. One red, one green, and one blue bubble of various sizes, though each big enough to fit the bottom of a glass, mug, or even small bottle, which gives Cookie the coaster concept. It makes sense to portray the band name within the red, center, sphere, but how now to do so gives way to complications. Twisting the phrase around itself in a circular fashion to appear like a cake, retrogressive to the kitchen though that might be, is surely appealing. Only it proves unreadable, no matter how much Hans Floral Nightingale argues otherwise. Having the three words curved one along the inside top of each orb is an option, though this implies that the bubbles would then become part of the logo, blowing up to who knows what. It is here that Hans Floral Nightingale has what he has no qualms about describing as 'a hemorrhaging of genius'. He had been staring intently at the fourth Led Zeppelin album long into the night, not for the first time considering that Buttery Cake Ass too should take on their own symbols for each band member. The essential problem being, for him anyway, that his own initials contain neither a B, a C, or an A, and he doubts that a bibbed cyan amaryllis or a bejewelled canary perched open-mouthed upon an anchor will much mitigate this fact. Secretly envying Max Beta who could easily use a chard leaf threaded through a film projector. But sometime during the witching hour, his eyes once again fall on Sandy Denny's rune of the three connected triangles. Searching about his room for a feather pen as a tribute to Robert Plant, although he's certain he most definitely does not possess any jars of ink, soon settling for a stick of charcoal, Hans sketches out the words Buttery Cake Ass running downwards à la Sandy Denny, fitting the design, with some not wholly undesirable effort, into the outline of a triangle, itself a sort of soft subtle arrow. The 'Ass' is on the bottom, the foundation, with the other two balanced on top, keeping in line with the whole Floorist philosophy. Hans places the new form within the central circle and is immensely satisfied with how it looks. There is also the keen sensation of pleasure as he notes that along with the three primary colours of light, they will henceforth be employing the holy trio of basic shapes - the square of their being a four piece, the circle of the Cake, and now the triangle-based logo. The others, when he brings it in the next day, all sense they have found what they've been looking for.

All of this was set on a lovely rich granite grey, and you can't shoot an arrow into that. As Cookie described all this, I found myself wonderin' if these unconnected circles and the archery-repellent background symbolized, maybe unconsciously, some sort of rift between Walter and the group? Maybe they resented gettin' their music out there at all? Be careful what you wish for, because it certainly is impossible to find. But I kept my mouth shut. Because why would you be in a band in the first place if you didn't want people to hear it? Though almost everything we'd learned about Hans Floral Nightingale so far pointed to such curmudgeonly behavior. And anyways Cookie was using other 7"s as coasters too. Even thinking of marketing the idea, but couldn't be bothered about the copyrights. Somewhere along the way - at one in the procession of shared apartments she inhabited - her copy of *Formaldehyde Hydro!* got left behind. The vinyl inside at any rate rendered unlistenable from thousands of tea cups, beer cans, and wine glasses coming down without proper care.

Trig and I marvelin' at how someone could be so nonchalant about a record they had been personally thanked on, and such a legendary one at that. For indeed this - after much travail and error - was how we found her. Spending so much time with the *Formaldehyde Hydro!* 7" that very first night as he taped it over and over again, turning the sleeve in his hands even exponentially more times, Fred had memorized its every detail. Though there was precious little information. No writing or recording credits, just the song titles, their lengths in parentheses, and a short thank you list. And tucked in between the names of Walter Graph City and Eric Dolphy was one Cookie Doone.

So we set about it systematically again, going to the library and taking out the phonebooks for every major metropolitan area in the country to assiduously scroll through, which at times seemed almost as time-consuming as visiting every graveyard and looking for a tombstone with a reference to Buttery Cake Ass. I reckon one of the advantages of being dead is that you don't have to make, or take, any calls. Only later did we realize that our difficulties were due to us starting with A and going alphabetically through the states, but there was always the chance we'd hit gold in California if she had made her way out to Hollywood to try her hand at the silver screen. It was a long slog through half the alphabet, though you soon fall into a rhythm, instinctively flipping the pages open to the DO section and scanning down for any C Doones. It was highly unlikely that 'Cookie' was on her birth certificate, so we looked for Catherine, Katharine, or even Caitlin. Anything which might permutate to, we were guessing, Katie and then a short hop, skip, and a jump on to what everyone knew her as. To be safe, we even peered a little further down the lists for Madeleine. Dial M For Cookie, ya know? Then it was finding an appropriate hour or two to call these numbers when someone might be home to answer. Trig working overtime to be able to afford the long distance charges. Not minding so much, his desire to obtain *Live In Hungaria* and now *Formaldehyde Hydro!* too great to be stopped by anything short of having his ears ripped off in some sort of thermonuclear explosion, and even then he'd still wanna see the covers, feel the vinyl in his hands, to know, however incompletely, what it had all been about. But these additional costs did put a dent in his record buying budget for a while, having to hold off on Need To Read's *Cassette Insert*, Rock Rock Rock N Roll's *Rock Rock Rock Rock N Roll*, Crowded Crevice's *Dynamite Hop*, and numerous other gems until the phone bills were paid. But it was all worth it when, having traversed the mountain of M's to come to the last of the 'New' states, we finally confirmed one C Doone who had known the band to be residing in Brooklyn. A wave of euphoria like neither of us had ever felt before swept through our souls as we stared at each other from across Trig's parents' living room, I grasping the receiver from the kitchen with both hands as twenty feet away Trig protruded over the upstairs railing having stretched his bedroom phone cord as far as it would go. Our hard work had paid off. Cookie's charm was evident from her first word and greater still as she continued, for after we had asked the all-important, life-changing, opening question 'Are you the Cookie Doone who is thanked on Buttery Cake Ass' *Formaldehyde Hydro!* 7"?', before she even responded in the affirmative, Trig and I just sensing this was the one, well, the two of us temporarily lost the capacity to speak and smell for about 15 seconds. Not that the latter one has anything to do with it, but it was an odd experience, especially with Trig's mom having left one of her ever-fragrant cinnamon apple pies to cool on the table, fresh out of the oven as it was, as we prepared for this most momentous of phone calls. The crisp delicious scent hitting us once again as the voice on the other end of the line giggled 'Hello?...Hello?' in what we couldn't be certain wasn't an imitation of John Lydon on PiL's partially eponymous first single. Then echoing Fred's 'It's been a long time since I've heard that name.', shocking us that Buttery Cake Ass weren't still, so many years later, a vibrant part of her everyday life.

The conversation was - barring her playing *Live In Hungaria* down the phone line and then sending us that very copy - everything we could have hoped for. Giving us an overview of the early history (presented above) and even offering that we should look her up if we were ever in New York. Although she told us she didn't have copies of the records, had lost touch with anyone who might, and had no idea where else one might obtain them, Trig and I took her up on this invitation straight away. Trig quickly improvisin' that we would actually be in The Big Apple in three weeks' time and would of course love to meet her. A date was set, an address given, and, when we hung up, a trip was to be planned.

Trig continuin' to work overtime until the minute we left, comin' off a 16 hour double shift and thinkin' he'd take the wheel. I vetoed this right away by grabbin' the keys, though this meant havin' to deal with him claimin' to psychically sense records the whole long drive to NYC. That feeling as I shifted into gear was one of the most wonderful I have ever known. Here we were on the precipice of perhaps finally gettin' our hands on these Holy Grails. On the verge of gettin' it on. Though Cookie would later tell us, sittin' exactly 21 days later in her ultra-hip front room, that much as the boys loved Funkadelic, sharing with Walter a reverence towards the first three records in particular, Buttery Cake Ass didn't sound anything like George Clinton and the gang. She disclosed to us much else too, and we hastily lapped it up along with the tea and banana bread she served. Although Cookie claimed to be clueless as to where to find the records anymore, she herself admitted she'd never actually looked for them. But New York City and environs lay before us! And we'd always heard that NYC was packed with the most mind-blowin' music emporiums. We reckoned we'd need at least a week to hit every one of them. Even then we'd have to keep careful track of time, arrivin' when their doors opened and not leavin' until we were asked to. We stayed in a flea-ridden hostel where the sink looked like someone had died in it. Savin' additional money by acceptin' Cookie's offer of takin' the rest of the banana bread with us and then carefully rationin' it out over the course of our stay. Not forkin' out for anything else besides the Buttery Cake Ass releases, and any possible memorabilia, that we had put our hard-earned money aside for. Which was incredibly difficult, let me tell you. We found hundreds, nay, thousands, of records we wanted to bring home. Trig had earmarked $300 for *Live In Hungaria* alone. He was hopin' to procure it for less than that, but he'd spend all three bills if he had to. I knew it would then be up to me to come through with *Formaldehyde Hydro!* and anything else, that in those halcyon days we still believed, the band might have put out. Cookie set us straight on their discography, however. It would be just those two slabs of elusive plastic. And when, on that final day, we were still turnin' up Cake Ass empty, that $300 went lightnin' quick. The whole trunk of the car fillin' with vinyl faster than we could make room for it. Overflowin' into the records Trig kept up front to pore over - Jump Boy's *Trampolining Tower Of Pisa*, Deuce Leatherby's *Falconeering Gloves Of The Century*, and Mixolydian Harold's *Blow Hard Knights*, to name but three - and then all the cassettes and cds for the stereo on the drive home. Captain Beefheart's *Lick My Decals Off, Baby*, Smokey Mirrors' *I Want My Crack At The Title*, Peon Swimming's *Cannonball!*, and that was just the first two and a half hours. At Cookie's suggestion, we paused in our shoppin' to meet her at Benny's Burritos for a farewell lunch, this lovely woman treating then walkin' us to Adult Crash afterwards and tellin' us to keep in touch. When the shops closed that night, with what we hoped was enough money for gas in our pockets, we set off back home. As it was, we had to scour underneath, between, and within the seats for loose change when we saw a toll comin' up. Amazing as the trip had been, fillin' in so much missing information on this mythical band and the endless hours perusin' shops that seemed sent straight out of heaven, not a single one of them contained or had even heard of Buttery Cake Ass. That car ride home gripped us in the most intense battlin' emotions, the thrill of havin' a million new songs to listen to, of havin' met someone who had been in the same room with Hans Floral Anderson and Hans Floral

Nightingale, of the great adventure we had just made happen, all the while feelin' the full impact of havin' failed to obtain the object of our continuin' quest. Maybe if I was Gogol or Carlisle I could do justice to the ultimately wonder-tinged despair of it all. But I'm not.

Cookie told us it was sad when she went back to visit her hometown too. Trig and I assumin' there was probably some free dental care involved with her dad and all, her teeth were immaculate. Confessing she got misty driving by the old site of Graph City with those two shopfronts in the strip mall all boarded up, later finding out that the veterinarian who took over the premises was driven out of town for practicing without a license. Rumors running rampant that he just relied on old episodes of *Scooby Doo* and *The Smurfs*, successfully for some time it must be pointed out, as the townsfolk mostly only had cats and dogs.

Her father possessing a great deal of information about the situation when she asked him. Though this turned out to be simply pieces of the puzzle that would need further fitting together for any sort of conclusive answer, seeing as his patients gave him the deets whilst reclining with a plethora of surgical instruments protruding from their mouths. And his practice was hoppin'. Plenty of toothaches to fix in a day, a steady stream of customers like an unbroken strand of saliva hanging over the lip of the office doorway. Cookie's dad didn't have the time to stop and let them clarify what became of the record store owner who had put out the first Buttery Cake Ass 7". What the good doctor, who must have warned his clientele about the dangers of too many sweets, thought of such a name is another burnin' question Trig and I have for the man if we ever get to meet him.

When we'd finally finished at Goose Train - Trig and Fred's magnificent dance seeming to extend to the infinite - it was 6 o'clock in the morning. The parking lot completely empty. We'd stayed there all night. Thankfully Fred had taken further inspiration from Graph City and installed that soda pop fridge, and as we walked outside, the Sun just comin' up, armed with this vast amount of new intelligence, albeit not really any closer to actually hearin' Buttery Cake Ass, it was a feeling of 'alright, where to next?' The caffeine jitters keepin' the arms of sleep at bay. Held-off dreams sneakily ticklin' us with greater worlds to explore. What Trig desperately wished for on occasions like these was some sort of giant carousel, circlin' through all the record stores in a given area. With of course points, intersections, that you could then use to get you onto the next giant carousel. It's a given you'd be ridin' the horses, like the questing knights you were, that's half the fun of record shoppin'! Choose and book your steed ahead of time online these days. Have this network cover the whole United States, and then one day the world. Make it easy to get over to that Hapsburg Empire. Though I'm not suggestin' these carousels go back in time, I mean that'd be melon-twistin'. There is no timeline I know of where Buttery Cake Ass and Austro-Hungary co-existed. Or if they even had record shops back then. Wax cylinders, maybe. Perhaps a proto-Cake Ass coulda been tourin'. Stranger things have happened...

These giant nodal carousels, I guess you could use them for anything, not just record shoppin'. Though it makes sense to have that be the priority. Giant Carousel System vs The Internet. It'd be wise for a consortium of record shops to copyright the concept post-haste. But I mean it's Trig's invention! He should have ownership of it. With covered tops and see-through walls and doorways to give you both the complete carousel effect and protection from the elements. Rain and whatnot. As I've pointed out before, that stuff ain't sayin' nothin'. You gotta take on the weather at its own game. Even if it doesn't listen to you. Or rather simply doesn't respond, makin' you unsure if it's even heard ya in the first place. Stayin' but not sayin'. The mysteries of the universe, you know? But even if the weather report is heavy, under each wooden beast there'll be a huge chest to stash your records in. Or heck, put them in the chests of the horses themselves. They can open up, like the Tin Man for his heart, but for your bounty. Everything about this mode of conveyance is brilliant. I gotta hand it to Trig, he would sketch these designs out in art class in high school, during math too, under the guidance of that teacher who told him about stayin' up 72 hours straight. Plottin' the radii of the circles and all that. It's a grand old idea, why aren't these cities workin' on it? In a perfect world, maybe... Though presumably in a perfect world there'd already be record stores on there so you'd never have to get off the carousel. Speaking of which, brings us to the departure of one Hans Floral Nightingale...

Cookie provided us with some insight into the whole band dynamic at the time, poised as she was to see it all clearly. The intergroup workings going much deeper than seven inches. That those who did hear the *Formaldehyde Hydro!* single, especially those who pronounced it correctly, thought the Jekyll & Hyde reference pointed to a rift between the two Hans Florals. That, living and breathing Buttery Cake Ass 24-7 like they did, the two had become almost interchangeable, even to each other. And now that they'd at last found a name that expressed their identity, trying to reclaim that of their own left each pretty disoriented. There were long talks, with even longer silences. You know how young men are, trying to express, well, anything to each other. Heck, on this quest Trig and I even experienced a little of that. I told you how I wasn't entirely on board with the whole stayin' up 72 hours straight to gain the spiritual insight he claimed was necessary to find the records...

At that first gig without Hans Floral Nightingale, as a trio no less, the band has to deal with the rumors abounding, though perhaps 'abounding' is too strong a word, but the questions being asked - is Hans going solo? Attendance at the second and third post-HFA gigs is very sparse, even less than what they are used to, as if Hans Floral Nightingale had been the attraction, his argumentative nature serving to pull those early hangers-on in, and now that he wasn't there, neither were they. Or perhaps they went off to college. No one sees them around to ask. Although they had always been something of a nuisance, their presence is missed when it comes to playing to near-empty rooms.

And then one day he just disappears. Again like that Madness song...

What became of the great Hans Floral Nightingale, 'inestimable' as he was? No one knows for sure. People have conjectured that maybe he ended up impersonating a stone wall inside unsuspecting pet stores. Or that he constructed triangular tables, for a while. No one ever bothering to postulate that maybe, just maybe, he really did become a florist. Hiding in plain sight! As so many of them are wont to do.

However, there are those who say that shortly before he left Buttery Cake Ass, Hans Floral Nightingale heard tale of a mythical Ramones free jazz album, and went off in search of such treasure. Never coming back. And there are those who will tell you he actually did find it.

This idea of the Ramones free jazz album - recorded right there in New York City, the Ramones' hometown, truly having it all, where free jazz flourishes amongst a wide variety of flower shops, Trig and I can confirm - well, it was like they simply sidestepped into a different dimension. One tantalizingly close and parallel to ours, coming back with tapes of a whole new sound, which in turn sparked a local punk jazz scene. Nothin' like what Jaco was layin' down on Weather Report's *Mr. Gone*. More 'jazz' in the accumulation of sound. And noise, and fury. Propping up melodies derived from their deep felt love of pop, or so I'm told, though I've also been told that's not it at all, that perhaps the closest you could come to describin' this new music was by way of a triangular table.

Before he vanishes, Hans Floral Nightingale shares this vital information with Hans Floral Anderson, and the beginnings of a new direction for Buttery Cake Ass take root. HFN expressing to HFA that he wishes for them to carry it on, what they'd started together... Of course with their wide musical sensibilities, even when it does come close to sounding like free jazz, Hans Floral Anderson can be heard shouting interjections of 'second verse, same as the first'. Despite there being no discernable framework to the tune. With the oblique smile on Hans Floral Anderson's face, one can never tell if this is a joke on his part or just supreme pleasure in the music they are making, seeing designs no one else does. Word still circulates that if you had witnessed the band rehearsing around this time, it would've been the most mindblowing sonic attack you'd ever hope to encounter, but that the one time they tried to record this on a boombox in the garage, the tape came out completely blank. So in an effort to appease the spirits of audio technology, they revert to writing more structured, well, what might be thought of as 'songs'.

What is Hans Floral Nightingale doin' now? The question persists. Perhaps it seems obvious, in hindsight at least, that with -hyde and Hydro, Hans Floral Nightingale would go into hiding. Some say that he just sits in a room all day, living solely within its four walls, one of which is a giant aquarium. No one knows if there's anything in it, not even water. Which gets us into the debate - can it be considered an aquarium if there's no water, no *aqua*, in it? Beware Counterfeit Aquariums, ya know. I mean, fools, prophets, and philosophers have argued over this for centuries. And I'm not sure if there's a satisfactory resolution. I think you can prolly have your own opinion. The subject certainly makes for lively discussion. Though I haven't the faintest idea if you can marry inter-faith with this. If someone believes an empty tank is still an aquarium and your family doesn't, I think that's just askin' for trouble. Down the line, at least. It might be overshadowed by the romantic sparks at first, especially if you've spent the last six years of your life alone in a room with only an empty aquarium for company. To then finally find someone with whom you truly connect - on every point except this one - and even if upon meeting their parents they keep silent about their true feelings that it's not really an aquarium if there's nothing in it, eventually the issue is gonna rear its ugly head. And I know what you're sayin', that if there's no water, then where is it rearin' from? Well, believe me, I get it.

But when the Cake Asses are able to recover and regroup, adding a member to bring them back up to the hallowed four-piece, well, now the time is ripe. They are ready to make *Live In Hungaria*.

PART THREE - IN GRADIENTS

Enter the radical guitar stylings of one Hubert 'Strings' Stringfellow, now operating under the name Blish Billings, a perfectly reasonable reaction to someone suggesting he go by 'Huey Longstraw'. But from the moment he strode into the Cake Ass' world, he was Blish. That's not to say we should turn our backs on his original handle as it was what made him pick up the instrument in the first place, though perhaps not for the reasons one might think. If your name is Stringfellow, you might think that your fate is fixed, and Blish, well, Blish was a big believer in free will, from a young age too. That Rush song from a few years back just confirming it to him. He looked on any strings as competition - yo-yo's, shoelaces, kites - he was no one's puppet. But it was a constant battle to posit himself as the embodiment of string in this cord-heavy world. Still, Fate is a tricky overlord, a superconductor if you will, to life's infinite orchestra, and Blish was blinded to that old sense of predetermination as he felt himself drawn to master these things. Considering instead, their very existence to be a direct challenge to his own being. As a preteen he spent weeks locked away in the library, absorbing all he could about Ben Franklin, emerging to then launch kites into the loftiest of positions, unconcerned so much with their colours and shapes than as to what they were carrying, and how far he could fly a piece of string. Soon he was commanding ten yo-yo's at once, one for each finger and thumb, untroubled by the great clacking back into his hands. It seemed inevitable that one day he would approach the guitar in much the same way, and it was seeing a photo of Hendrix lighting his Strat on fire that convinced him there was something in this. Growing up in the 70s was a good time for any would-be axemen as their aspirational kind were revered as giants in the music world. Of course Blish's ear was drawn to a few of them - John McLaughlin, Sonny Sharrock, Zoot Horn Rollo... In the early 80s, now of the same age as the rest of the Cake Asses - you know what I mean, he was always the same age as them, but here he was too - and in the early 80s where we have just been traveling through with the other members, Blish was fortunate enough to get his hands on some of those Birthday Party albums. Rowland S. Howard's playing blowing Blish's mind. Well, I guess he was still Hubert then, but same rules apply...

Blish hailed - if you want the alliteration you can say 'Hubert hailed', or 'Huey hailed', some people did call him Huey occasionally, which he preferred a lot more than Strings, with its plural, he wanted to be *the* String, resenting the authorities who told him otherwise - well, this gentleman came from about 40 miles north of Buttery Cake Ass Central, as the crow flies. Or any bird, really. Or if we're talkin' about a food fight we could say 'as the cake flies'. Even if we're not speakin' of such matters, can you imagine throwin' a piece of cake 40 miles? What an Olympic event that would be! But you can't have a food fight coverin' so much acreage. Well, you could, but it's not the polite thing to do. Too many unsuspecting casualties. Because even if you could throw a piece of cake one single mile, your sense of aim ain't gonna be that precise. Same for throwin' a handful of M&Ms eight miles. Who knows what you'll hit. And settin' up catapults might be too disruptive to county activities. You'd never get the permits...

However! Attaching a piece of cake to an arrowhead will give you the accuracy you require. And so perhaps it was no coincidence that Blish Billings headed straight to Graph City Records and its accompanying archery emporium when he left his hometown carrying just his guitar and a small bag on his back.

Why he chose this particular destination is unclear. Blish claims to never have previously heard the *Formaldehyde Hydro!* 7", nor Buttery Cake Ass, or of them in any of their current or previous incarnations. But one day Walter finds him sleeping underneath the pinball machine, that area being wide open at the time, not yet used for storage. Again no one knows how long he was sneaking in at night to get some rest, but Walter sees the guitar case and, sympathetic soul that he is, lets Blish slumber on. Taking a quick look about the shop to make sure nothing is missing, which it isn't. When Blish wakes up, Walter is quick to offer him some breakfast and as the final bite is swallowed, asks to hear him play. Dragging an amp over from the archery side of the premises, having rescued it from an irate father threatening to use it as target practice if his son didn't turn the volume down. And when Blish plugs in, well, this is music Walter has longed to hear. It quickly enters his mind that in combination with Hans Floral Anderson's burgeoning talent the two could really do something special together.

Walter is of course well aware that the Cake Asses now needed some fresh blood. Hans Floral Nightingale's sudden departure leaving everyone quite unanchored and Walter sitting on nearly 100 *Formaldehyde Hydro!* 7"s to sell. Walter is also privy to the knowledge that Hans Floral Anderson is spending more and more time locked up at home, perpetually brooding over his predicament. Getting this info straight from the horse's mouth, as drummer Max Beta has taken to warming up his wrists at the old pinball machine before rehearsals, asking Walter to throw on The Who's *Tommy* and playing along. Explaining over the thwacks and chings how Hans Floral Anderson has been a shell of his former self these weeks since the tornado hit. The trio obviously isn't working. Any similarities to Cream or ZZ Top are in name only, all sensing something is missing. A something Hans has grave doubts about ever being able to be replaced. He isn't sleeping much, and writing Cookie long letters as she too left town shortly after Hans Floral Nightingale's disappearance. Luckily Cookie saved these missives. Their contents are concerning. Consistent throughout the diatribes is the dilemma of how would he ever find someone again who understood the whole Floorists worldview. An additional puzzle piece necessary to help him achieve what Hans Floral Nightingale had saddled him with - the soaring into the horizons illuminated by the legend of the lost Ramones free jazz album. Not to mention someone to fill the musical space underneath when he blazes into an abacus solo. Perhaps in an attempt to entice Hans Floral Nightingale back into the fold via supernatural means, the letters of the BCA logo have begun to bulge again, a quite literal spell. Not the thickset triptychs they once were, but Hans Floral Anderson has been adding lines left and sometimes right.

Walter sees a succession of solutions stretching out before him and begins to make arrangements. Offering the space underneath the pinball machine for Blish's continued slumber, even giving him employment delivering archery supplies and manning the other counter when the shops get full. With Hans Floral Anderson it would be a little more complex. Walter knows how it is with most creative types, you can't approach them head on. So like the puppet master Blish Billings both fears and sees himself as in equal measure, Walter sets about orchestrating what in a nineties film about the Seattle grunge scene might be called a 'meet cute'.

Not having to wait long for an excuse to phone Hans Floral up and get him down to Graph City as, with Blish supervising the shops, at the weekend's record convention Walter finally scores a copy of Nigel Dinks' *Drinks With Dinks*. An LP he knows Hans Floral Anderson is dying to hear, especially as it is the definitive recording of Dinks' quintet with Alan Wilforn on flugelhorn, recorded at the end of their 1971 stint in Vienna. Having learned from Max Beta that there would be no rehearsal that evening, it being Davey Down's mother's birthday, Walter smoothly dials Hans Floral's number and gives him the news, telling him he'll be open late that night and to come on in anytime. Meanwhile paying Blish overtime restocking shafts and quivers in the room next door.

When he sees Hans rounding the far bend into the parking lot, Walter calls Blish back into the record shop, dropping the needle on side two of *Drinks With Dinks*. Knowing that along with everything else, Blish's ears would be poppin' to Gus Falloway's drumming on Malaise Maze, Falloway sounding just like a Minotaur in a chemistry lab, as allegedly were Dinks' instructions for the track. Blish standing there grooving to it as Hans walks through the door, recognizing it right away although he's never heard it before, only read a review in an obscure English-language Berlin fanzine, *Upstairs At Vince's*.

The music drawing the two young men closer as it would from that point on, and when they eventually do speak, both looking up at the same time to acknowledge the wild fury of Gibby Fitzgregory's fuzzed out Fender Rhodes, they immediately click. Even more immediately, if such a thing is possible, work then begins on the legendary *Live In Hungaria* album. Not in any tangible sense of course, the two haven't even learned each other's names yet, but again with the mysticism that would wind its way around the band from time to time, it is here - to any discerning puppeteer - that the idea of that monumental record drops its seed into the ether.

76

Walter soon introducing them after they've talked their way through a handful of Dinks-related recordings - 1968's *Invisible Dink*, Alan Wilforn's spotlight piece, Wilfully Forlorn, from Dinks' 1970 follow-up *In A Pensive Mood*, and Fitzgregory & Falloway's own foray into rock with *ff*, a record Hans had only gotten his hands on last month. The two getting further acquainted long into the night. Walter sticking around, pretending to go over the books as he eavesdrops, sporadically tidying up, and when the time comes, nonchalantly moving Blish's guitar to within Hans' line of sight. The Cake Ass front man giving a little jolt, 'Walter, you started selling instruments?' Walter kindly smiling, nodding towards Blish.

Hans doesn't ask Blish to play, nor hears him do so that night. Though when he learns that his new friend has been sleeping underneath Graph City's pinball machine, Hans thinks this might be someone he could get his own place with, so large is their common love of records completely obscure to the rest of the world. With Cookie now gone, Hans is wanting more than ever to find a place of his own. But also with there being no mattress, nothing, Blish bedding down straight onto the hard wood in just a bag, just to be able to be close to the music, Hans Floral Anderson believes this dude might just get the whole Floorists concept. And with his name starting with a B, could symbolize a much-needed new beginning for Buttery Cake Ass... Hans wastes no time in inviting Blish down to the next rehearsal.

It is magic from the first note, as Hans describes to Cookie in a letter. She was livin' it up in New York City, occasionally finding the time in her hectic social life to write Hans back. In one hastily jotted dispatch even gushing about a new artist she's been seeing live who she just knows is gonna be huge. Hans, intrigued, quickly fires off a response instructing Cookie to give this 'Madonna' her personal copy of *Formaldehyde Hydro!* and ask if she'd like Buttery Cake Ass to come to New York and open for her some time. He'll naturally send Cookie another 7" as a replacement. When we read this part of the letter out loud, Cookie can't stop gigglin'. By this time, the record in question has been scratched to smithereens, Cookie realizin' that a 7" single can yield two coasters - the sleeve and the vinyl itself. Her front room contains a good number of these, Trig and I usin' Tin Tin's Toast And Marmalade For Tea and Rupert Holmes' Escape (The Piña Colada Song) respectively.

At the first get-together the band don't play any of the Cake Ass material that Hans Floral Nightingale had a hand in writing. It doesn't seem fair to either Hans or Blish. And besides, creativity is flowing like water, like cake batter, and not watery cake batter. After just a week of rehearsals, they have enough new ideas to fill up two 90 minute cassettes, playing for hours in that garage, losing themselves to all notions of time, except for what Max Beta is laying down on the kit. Over the following five days these demos are reworked further, edited down into a single 'best of' cassette.

Trig, though salivatin', knew the likelihood of ever coming across one of these was probably even a negative percentage, seein' how difficult it was to find the official releases. But that didn't stop his mind from reelin' at what might be on those tapes.

Soon some of this stuff is deemed good enough to bring down to Walter to hear. The compositions are out there but still within the bounds of the boombox being able to capture them, and the possibility of recording a full-length album begins to be excitedly bandied about. Something that was never actually the case with Hans Floral Nightingale. Perhaps further proof to the theory that he didn't want his music to be heard... Hans, Blish, Davey Down, & Max Beta on the other hand are now diving deep into discussions about what big labels would be up for signing them. While at the same time picking over that particular proclivity of soul that makes them also want the small obscure companies that handled some of their heroes to be involved in the distribution of their music. Although they aren't consciously aware of it, they know better than to ask Walter to put out another release on Graph City Records. Though once when all four are hanging out at the record store, talk again turns to signing with a major and its conversational counterpart - the dreaded accusation of selling out - Walter just smiles and plops a box of 50 *Formaldehyde Hydro!*s on the counter with the words 'you'd better worry about selling these first'.

Walter realizing that the boys need focus, that although what is coming out of the garage is indeed brilliant, if in fact their goal is to make a full-length album, even one which he won't be funding, that they should start shaping the wild sounds heard on those cassettes. Not taming, rather forming them into what would become a somewhat cohesive whole. In order to help them achieve their target, Walter installs them in the archery side of the premises, the concept of arrows and trick shots being perfectly in tune with Blish's style of guitar playing, so that the unit can rehearse under Walter's watchful ear. He keeps both shops open so that their practices become like a sort of performance art, customers treated to a steady stream of live shows. Though it must be said, try as we might, Trig and I could not find anyone who had ever been to one. Which is odd. I mean, imagine if you're an archery enthusiast and you go to purchase a new drawstring or whatever - I don't know how these things work, is it like dental floss? does it run out? if only we could get in touch with Cookie's dad... - but you go to this shop and while you're scannin' its wares for what you want to buy, you're surrounded by the outrageous musical stylings of a band called Buttery Cake Ass? Surely you'd be talkin' about it to this day! Hans described such conundrums to Cookie in his letters, his disappointment that it wasn't winning them over any fans. Not one invitation to any sort of archery convention, nothing. But on the plus side it was making them a much more cohesive unit, and he details how Walter took care of them, even bringing in food so they could eat. Onlookers watching the group descend on these victuals like a pack of starving jackals, a sight not incongruent with but apparently overshadowing the group's performances of a more musical nature.

One evening when Walter is out picking them up some pizzas *sans* the *fromage*, Blish keeping an eye on the customers between blistering guitar work - 'ripping', as Hans Floral Anderson puts it on more than one occasion - the Cake Asses collectively receive the idea to mic up the pinball machine. Agog at this revelation, they set about doing so, positively walking on air with excitement. Walter coming back, putting the za's down and calmly explaining to the eager Asses that Faust had already done this on their first UK tour in '73. Although the band are crushed for the remainder of the evening, eating those cheeseless za's with no zest whatsoever, it does save them from the increasingly tiresome argument about adding a further member to play yet another new instrument. And also from having to transport a giant pinball machine which Walter definitely doesn't want moved from the store in the first place - think of the TILTS! - something not possible anyways in Max Beta's Datsun Cherry, that you'll remember has trouble even fitting the boys in.

The music pinged by the machine is not lost, however. In fact, it is incorporated into the hyper and hypnotic groove that will make up the first number on *Live In Hungaria* - the 12 minute opus, Artchery. Spelled like Art Cherry but cherry with only one R, so like archery but art, ya know? And cherry. So it's like one word smushed together like an ice cream sundae, with that little red fruit on top. But in this case at the end. And like I said, with only one R. Seein' the title written down this should all be obvious.

Artchery is Max Beta's baby, really. The pinball portion, anyway. He would use the rehearsal tapes as the tune materialized, arriving early to band practice, throwing 'em on the stereo and starting to work out parts. Quite a cool rhythmic design, though one which, much to Max's chagrin, Hans Floral Anderson would later play on the recording. The group having captured Artchery live with Hans getting his guitar to play on via an echo unit, moving over to the mic'd up metal monster and letting fly a perfect recreation of what Max has put his whole soul into bringing into being. Trying to be fair, and aware that a band is at least an *attempt* at democracy, Hans lets Max try to overdub his contribution later, muting the channels which Hans has recorded on. Luckily they had set up the space perfectly to avoid much bleed through. But it just doesn't have the same magic as that initial take, and everybody knows it. His disappointment and frustration over this forming the basis of the one letter Max ever wrote to Cookie...

With Artchery, everything is coming together. Their daily run-throughs in an archery/music shop and the concept of trying to get a pinball machine into Max Beta's car, the Datsun Cherry, the silver ball of said machine the very art cherry implied by the title. This fruit that they had previously had so much difficulty working into the C of their name, blossoming here in such a nurturing environment, its time having finally arrived. Buttery Cake Ass even hoping 'Artchery' might bestow itself upon a new musical genre. Like how Krautrock was the opening track on side one of *Faust IV*. And of course without people then concluding that the cake is cherry-flavoured, or even accompanied by cherry ice cream like Duran Duran would later have you believe.

We're gettin' a bit ahead of ourselves and I hope I haven't given too much away. Spoiler alert! Actually, the phrase 'spoiler alert' wasn't in use back then on account of it not havin' been invented yet. Or maybe it was? Apparently it was first used in 1982, when all this was going on. Not said in relation to Buttery Cake Ass, but to that crazy Star Trek film *The Wrath Of Khan*. Spoiler alert, I guess, if you didn't know that! Though I'm sayin' this after the fact so it isn't really much of an alert. What would it be then? 'Spoiler pointing out possibly too late but maybe not', in case your interlocutor didn't pick up on what was revealed? And while we're at it, has there ever been a *Wrath Of Khan* con? A convention dedicated solely to that movie... But the phrase 'spoiler alert' was written on Usenet, that early internet discussion group, and the term most likely hadn't reached anyone even remotely associated with Buttery Cake Ass. But *Wrath of Khan*, with that crazy thing in his ear?! It'd be hard to argue with anyone supposing there were links between the two... Though perhaps you might have deduced by the title itself that *Live In Hungaria*...was recorded live...

It just so happens that a friend of Blish's is visiting from his hometown. One Reginald 'Baton' Button. Who, if he was gonna be credited on records, had a difficult choice to make. For he loved that his nickname 'Baton' could be viewed as simply a different pronunciation of Button. But that it could also be a literal baton. Like in the relay races that he never ran. Or the sticks one twirls, that he never did. Or the conductor's wand for a musical orchestra that he had enough of a sense of shame to know that you can't pull that sort of stunt in a studio with a bunch of rock musicians. But this was what he wanted to do with his life - engineer some records. And he has been buying up equipment back home to do so.

Reg and Blish - or rather 'Strings' as Reg Baton initially calls him, to some confused looks from the band, they then assuming it is because of his guitar prowess - the two of them sharing the sleeping space underneath the pinball machine, talking long into the night about the music they would each make, touring the world, levitating audiences with it... The following day the Cake Ass are hanging around Graph City before rehearsal, chatting about the tunes and how much they are itching to get recording but perplexed as to how they might accomplish this. Reg Baton listening and then suggesting 'Why don't you just do it here?' All raising their eyebrows at the idea, five expectant faces then turning to Walter, who would have the only say worth mattering in this discussion. To which after a moment's consideration he replies, 'Why not?' It seemed to make sense, as they had all their stuff right there. Including the pinball. The use of which Max still naively believes will fall to him.

Reg Baton jumping in the deep end fully clothed now, telling them he could do it. Keeping to himself that it's the chance he's been waiting for. He'll just bring his gear down and set up. Everything could stay in place as it was. The discussion moving on to the Rolling Stones' famous mobile recording studio that they used for *Exile On Main Street*. Walter finding a sense of cosmic justice in this as his shop had originally been located *on* Main Street when he first came to town, before the rents got to it, driving him to the outskirts. Then mentioning that that studio had been used to record The Who's Won't Get Fooled Again, tying it all back to pinball machine music. Max Beta growing overly excited, too amped up to suggest with any degree of politeness that Reg Baton & Blish's sleeping arrangements will need to be shifted in order to mic the game up properly. And is promptly comforted by Reg Baton's 'of course', sounding aghast that they might do anything different. Perhaps the more cynical among us might also take Won't Get Fooled Again as part of Walter's feelings towards funding a new album. Though such a view doesn't hold water considering how encouraging Walter has been, providing the band with food, shelter, and a place to practice. He would even be bankrolling these recordings, with the idea to license them to a new label and hopefully get some of his investment back with somebody else having to figure out how to sell them.

Further conversation about the Stone's studio-in-a-truck reveals to the boys that four classic Zeppelin albums were also recorded using it, which may account for the rumors of occultish goings on with the Cake Ass too. Speaking of pinball machine music, later that year Lou Reed will use the very same mobile unit to record his *Live In Italy*. But no one was to know that at the time...

As the plans begin to be laid, talk around the shop often turns to live albums. I guess there was a great amount of innocence floating through the world back then, with everyone continuing to trust that KISS' *Alive!* would fall into this category. The band digs the MC5's *Kick Out The Jams*, with its own allusion to food, and Iron Maiden's *Maiden Japan* they think just looks rad. The Ramones *It's Alive* - no free jazz in sight, or whatever the aural equivalent is, no matter how close you put your ears to the record. Blish postulating what if Joey, Dee Dee, and co. had covered the entire KISS album? And then all the jazz recordings - Eric Dolphy's *In Europe*, Miles with *Live-Evil* and *Dark Magus*, and of course Nigel Dinks' plethora of releases - *Everything But The Kitchener Dinks (Live In Ontario 1967)*, *Skating Dink (Live at Olympiahalle, Innsbruck, Austria 1977)*, *Nigel At The Gates Of Evening (Live in Floyd, New York 1968)*, etc.

And although the official title of the record is *Cheap Trick At Budokan*, the Cake Ass and their cohorts are no different from most in referring to it as 'Live At Budokan', a switch-up which will prove prescient. For it is decided that there should be a run-through to test everything out, Reg Baton hightailing it home and coming back with a van full of electronics. Walter deeming it best to close the shop that Saturday so that any customers won't interfere with the recording process. Truth be told, the strategy of Buttery Cake Ass playing to the archery appurtenance buying public hasn't really panned out as well as he thought.

While waiting for Reg to come back and then setting up his equipment, they have records on for inspiration. 'Live At Budokan', *Drinks With Dinks*, *Skating Dink*, and *BooDinkspest (Live In Budapest Halloween 1969)*. Thinking how live albums should have that exotic feel. Even though they themselves can't afford to leave town. The closest they could probably come would be to go back to that bowling alley where most of the crowd got their name wrong... While getting the mic placements right, they are throwing around titles, playing on those of Cheap Trick and Nigel Dinks' various ensembles, eventually coming up with 'Live At Bootycon'. Which is the most likely source for the bootleg that soon starts circling around, *Live At Bootylicious*. Rumor has it this is the warm up for *Live In Hungaria*, where they were testing out the set-up the night before. Testing themselves too. Not, it should be clarified, that the archery side of Graph City was ever rebranded Bootylicious or Hungaria or even anything like that. At best, doing so would just be confusing to any would-be arrowheads. Suboptimal for business.

Such is the notoriety of the *Live At Bootylicious* cassette, that connoisseurs will tell you its title is completely apt. The band were all diggin' what this new artist called Prince was doing at the time. And despite this bootleg being completely blank, there is a quality to the air on it that will get anyone who listens in the mood quick as look-at-ya. Obviously there have been a number of issues over the years with bootlegs in general, which is tough because *Bootylicious* was already a bootleg. There's no legal copyright or anything. But, according to Fred, scoundrels have been known to try to sell tapes that are *not* a copy of the True Source. Passin' off blank cassettes as if they were Cake Ass gold. Of course aficionados can tell. But it's not like Buttery Cake Ass ever had any demand to make authenticating or going after the dishonest bootleggers a profitable enterprise for anyone. We can only surmise what a huge operation this would be if they had sold millions. *Bootylicious* might even get an official release...

That first night, with the test run, is harrowing. As with the problems the boombox faced in the garage, if 'problem' could be said to accurately describe this and not 'cosmic intervention', the sounds they are laying down are too conniving to be committed to tape. Like a slippery squirrel. But Reg Button, talkin' to us over the phone from his current studio, told us it was really something to behold, simply to be in the room that night. 'You can *feel* it on the tape.' Going on to explain that we can sense much more than we can hear. A big reason why he still eschews digital technology.

Reg setting to work immediately trying to figure out what's going so wrong, and there isn't much time to play with, having to be back at his day job on Monday morning. The weekend recording date Cookie even thought had been divined by astrological consultation. Though for what end, I am not sure. Without hearing it, I mean maybe *Live In Hungaria* is the masterpiece we hope it to be. I doubt they requested the star reader find them the perfect conjunction of the heavens for their album to be beset by technological headaches and then upon release become one of the most difficult to find in the history of recorded music, causing the group to fade into the sorrowful depths of obscurity... But if that had been the case, then well done.

Reg working through the night, the band themselves eventually heading home to get some rest before trying again. Blish, with his bed under the pinball machine, having to find somewhere else within the shop that wouldn't interfere with the microphone set-up. Reg Baton finally capturing some sounds in the wee hours, he and Blish then bunking down foot to foot behind the counter. Walter opening the shop late the next day to allow them their much needed sleep. Although there's only so long you can hold off early Sunday morning archery enthusiasts...

But perhaps there was something to that date after all, which I hope is written somewhere on the record. The closest we can pinpoint is sometime in the first half of 1983. Cookie's letters don't narrow it down much and Reg was so busy writin' recording notes he didn't have time in those days to scribble much else. As Fate would have it, Becca stops in the shop that afternoon claiming she doesn't have much to do, was just driving by, hasn't seen the boys in a while. Hans Floral Anderson having the clarity of mind to ask her to duet with him on the one tune for which he still feels unprepared. This is quite the thing. Although Becca herself was unaware that her friends had suggested her as the original vocalist for the band way back when, even before they were known as Bringing Carrots Auspicious, it was her name that had inspired the whole she-bang, long before Blish was ever involved.

The tune in question being The Most Wonderful Secret In The World. A phrase that Hans had written in his notebook late one night from the Jean Seberg film *Bonjour Tristesse*. Blish taking a tangent on the Francophilia by laying down a blissed out Richard Pinhas-esque guitar storm. Subtle and tasteful, suiting the song perfectly, though you wouldn't expect anything else from Blish Billings. And again with these cosmic coincidences, that title - The Most Wonderful Secret In The World - seemed to consign their fate thusly. To all of us at least, you included, that are privy to this tale.

They run through the song a couple times with Becca so she can familiarize herself with it and then ask her to come back at 8 that night after closing time when they are due to begin recording again. The session is to be treated as a live show. One that no one is really at, but that is no different to any of the gigs they've played so far. Another difference being the crucial move of stopping between takes to check and make sure the music actually sticks to the tape this time. Walter giving notes and directions, coaxing them into the correct mindset for each upcoming tune. A born record producer if there ever was one.

Reg Button describes The Most Wonderful Secret In The World as 'absolutely lovely, a brilliant performance from every member of the band, especially Becca. With her only having heard it for the first time that afternoon. And the perfect slot for it on the album too, the penultimate number on side B.' They couldn't have planned it any better. For although Hans said to come by at 8, she's been to their rehearsals at the old garage before and knows how these things work. Now entering through the Graph City doors at nearly 10 pm and still having to wait half an hour until they are ready for her. Reg recalls seeing Becca with her eyes closed mouthing along as the band record the backing track, each tune's vocals being cut immediately afterwards in a make-shift soundproof booth. Hans singing a guide for the others while they play, but of course he needs to be free to roam about the studio to cover the incidental pinball music and the like...

The songs are sung in English, there is no question about that, but Becca turns out to be a formidable chanteuse. Evocative of Françoise Hardy, Chantal Goya, France Gall, even a bit of Mina and Nina Brodskaya, ranging from breathy whisper on the wind to full-on roar of a tigress on the Russian steppe, and everything in between. One does wonder how Buttery Cake Ass would've panned out - no pun intended - if she had been there right from the beginning. As was almost the case. They nail the song first take. Walter insisting they move on, that they'd never get it, or possibly anything, that good again.

Furthering the French theme, though taking the music itself miles away from its original profundity, amongst Cookie's clique in New York, DJ Battery later made a 12" dance remix of Most Wonderful Secret called Let Them Eat Cake Ass. Cookie tells me this in confidence, not wanting to get Trig all worked up like he's been prone to do throughout our talks. A few unmarked white labels circulated for a week or two but the record was never officially pressed. She herself never even possessed a copy, the product having no coaster-like properties.

The second tune, what ends up being A Real Fridge In Real Life, takes a rather convoluted journey. At least title-wise. You see, Hans Floral Anderson had this idea. He'd heard the story about The Clash's version of Armagideon Time. How Kosmo Vinyl thought the perfect length for a single was 2 minutes 58 seconds, and so the group asked him to stop them when they got to that point. Look it up, there's all that banter on the track. Not that A Real Fridge In A Real Life sounds anything like Armagideon Time. According to Reg Button, anyway, who is tasked with halting the band when the clock reads 3 minutes and 14 seconds. Which, knowing the Clash story, he does not do. But we'll get to that...

The music did come about from just a song length though - yes, the aforementioned 3 minutes 14 - and is one of the first tunes they write with Blish. The perfect duration being a concept Hans Floral Anderson expended much mental energy upon. He considered 2:47 hard to beat for sheer aesthetic enjoyment, and of course the 3:33 trio of threes is pretty near immortal, except for the radio station standard of fading out at 3:30. 3:17 also has its own power, adding up to 11 as it does. It is no coincidence that 2:22 looks like a bevy of swans, for to contain a song within such short limits requires much grace and authority. 1:11 even trickier, but those upright numbers, resembling candles as they do, provide a beacon, brought all the closer by the explosion of punk rock. The day it finally comes to him, the group are standing around Graph City passing the import 12" of that first Cure record, *Three Imaginary Boys*, back and forth. The very real young men in the record store intrigued because when it was released in the States, the album had a different track listing and the title of *Boys Don't Cry*. They huddle over the sleeve, trying to figure out if the band are actually sobbing or not, and, as always, on the lookout for ideas to make into songs of their own. Someone soon putting forth - 'What would it sound like if we, Buttery Cake Ass, were in the refrigerator on the cover of this record?'

An intriguing proposition...

Hans holding the album a bit too long in his hands and starting to giggle. 'What if it was like a magic ice box...and turns us into pie?' Quickly snapping his fingers. 'We should do a song that's 3 minutes 14 seconds long!' They immediately write down that tempting song length, its temporary title just those three numbers. One digit separated from the other two by a colon, much like how a digestive tract would work in relation to Buttery Cake Ass' name.

Walter overhearing the whole conversation, now signals for them to hand him the record, dropping the needle on the song So What?, one of the tracks deleted from the US version. Watching mirthfully as the boys' eyes pop out at all the talk of cake in the lyrics. Which spurs them on in their intent for the new song, that a tune entitled 3:14 must be fated or something. The Cure offering them this refrigerator to crawl into and dare being somehow distorted into another dessert. Davey Down pointing out that the Cure themselves are almost a pi. Though with a slice taken out, making them only this fictional trio, three imaginary boys. Not that pi is an imaginary number, Davey clarifies. He had learned that at school.

After Cookie writes Hans back how annoying it is for him to keep referring to a song by only its time value, the boys start calling 3:14 'Magic Box'. Though they soon deem this title too risqué and thus begin writing it on the rehearsal set list as Buttery Pi Ass. Which really seems to sum it up. And is something Cookie has no response to. Then someone got lazy. One practice it is written with only a single S, reading simply PI AS. A mistake surely, but once again tying them to the great cinematic tradition. Those four letters standing in some circles for 'Play It Again Sam'. What he doesn't actually say in *Casablanca*...

It isn't until quite late in the game that the title is switched to what would wind up on the album - A Real Fridge In Real Life - with Brouce Cozzins, more on him later, Brouce Cozzins The Second obviously, initiating the fateful change. Brouce digs the concept behind the song, the Cure transforming this band from cake to pie like that, but feels a certain compulsion to suggest that while theme songs are always cool, this one is a bit confusing. Especially as it isn't, in fact, a theme song. With a debut album, clarity of vision is what is needed. Hans realizing that they haven't come this far in shaping their sense of identity only to jeopardize it with delusions of doppelgängers. And besides, with the 3 minutes 14 seconds listed on the sleeve, listeners might figure it out for themselves. Making the reference even more pure.

As it happens though, no one gets it. Not Brouce Cozzins The Second, not his father, not anyone. Being as, just like with the Clash, you can't stop time. No matter what Cher might have you believe. I assume you would have to stop time first in order to turn it back, and anyway Cher was gettin' ready for her acting career at this point. But like with the Clash - and as far as I know there are no films starrin' both Cher and The Clash, closest we get are the lyrics to Rock The Casbah - but the

Clash couldn't be stopped in time either, even with the word 'time' in the very title of the very tune they were tryin' to record...

After the victory that was the transcendent recording of Artchery, and all the excitement of getting that first track of their very first record down on tape, the boys are on a roll. Taking the music that eventually becomes A Real Fridge In Real Life to new levels, completely immersed in what they are doing, the spectral sounds emanating from their fingers like lavish lightning. To convey the original idea of the tune, the Graph City soda fridge is moved to directly face the band, its door propped slightly open and a microphone stuck in to capture the echo off its walls, as if the band were trapped in there. But as this process is morphing them, metaphorically at least, into another spectacular entity, the sound is anything but claustrophobic. At the three minute mark it still seems there is much more to spew forth. Walter and Reg Baton consulting and deciding to then stop them at 6:28, being roughly double the value of pi. Waving their arms around 6:20 to guide the group into the big finish. Listening back, the track is so hot, no one even cares about pi time. Though they do then stop to eat, to get their energy back up. Luckily the fridge has not been left open long enough to let anything spoil.

Up next is The Most Scathingly Brilliant Idea. The only Hans Floral Nightingale-era tune amongst the bunch. Completely reworked now with Blish, of course. But the title, coming as it does from the Hayley Mills film *The Trouble With Angels* that had been on tv early one Sunday afternoon when Hans and Hans were hanging out before the others came over to practice, has been around since they too had a wing-ed being in their name as Berzerker Carrot Angels. Whom you *would* expect trouble with, if not full-on mayhem. Both Blish and Hans choosing to play their guitars with actual carrots for the recording, each taking a verse, and in essence shredding the past. The physical evidence of which lays littering the floor. Walter shaking his head while stepping in to sweep up these string-sliced orange strips as soon as the final notes decay.

I know I mentioned that they had stopped to eat before undertakin' the recordin' of this one, but to be honest with you, who can say if they were tempted to chomp down those carrots thereby ruining all of this? Or if that was never even an issue, their integrity provin' much stronger than you might suppose for the average rock n roll musician. Anyway, this was a question Trig and I did not think to ask Reg 'Baton' Button when we had him on the phone, so caught up in the rest of the story we were receivin'. And to ring him back with such a query just seemed churlish. Although, like you, I'm dyin' to know...

The two songs whose titles were taken from films balanced in mirror image of each other as tracks three and seven on the album. The fact that each started with the words 'The Most' have led some to conjecture that they may have been trying to point out that their cake was moist, but without the egocentric 'I', displaying the strong united front that they were indeed a band.

An overall symmetry presented itself throughout, with four songs on each side. Which, yes, makes it a total of eight songs on the record. And I know what you're thinkin' - they ended up with the only number that is the past tense of eat, when they're called Buttery Cake Ass?! I agree, that's wild. And that fourth track on side one is a doozy, really going for the Ramones free jazz sound that Hans had promised Hans he would continue the quest for, although nothing on the album can really be said to sound much like The Ramones or free jazz at all. Hans Floral Anderson thinking it fitting to also tie this tune into what got him into music in the first place. The original concept that had brought him to this band that was now recording their debut album and felt unstoppable. That energy continuing into this fourth song entitled 13th Florist. Here Hans opting for only the one O to make it even more evocative. Lyrically setting this numbered flowerman up as a proponent of an anti-Floorists - that is with two O's - bent. Their own version of Parliament's Sir Nose D. Voidoffunk. And yes you would buy a nosegay from such a bouquet boutique, and smell it too. Hans explaining all that went into these lyrics and the whole Floorists bag to Reg Button on a car ride out to a later gig.

Opening up side two, Relics Of Forgotten Futures is perhaps the most devastating, pulverizing, song on the album. Conceived when thinking about a distant decade where no one could play pinball anymore, nuclear war and other apocalypti putting an end to this and other enjoyments, its place as track one side two ties it to the more positive Artchery, the ode to the game and machine that kicks off the record. Although every song appears to be connected to another, having a partner on the flipside, no mention of this was ever made by Hans or any member of the band. Reg could not recall even Walter, who was so integral to shaping the album, ever acknowledging this peculiarity. But Reg heard this as the structure, perhaps due to his role outside the Cake Ass as he was.

As the band were such experts with commenting on their previous band names, perhaps it was inevitable that they would one day do the same in song form. The tune following Relics Of Forgotten Futures, serious as that composition is, takes Relics' melody and contorts it like a balloon animal, and the type that require more than one party favour to make. Like a rhino or an elephant or a space giraffe. Wait a second, is it 'balloon animal' if it requires multiple balloons to construct? Shouldn't it be 'balloons animal'? But that doesn't quite sound right... And not quite sounding right is how track six, Crumbs, comes about. Walter encouraging the boys to run with it. Although they are keen on the notion of playing with form like this, doing so takes all their musical skill to wrangle. The popping sounds too having to be mic'd carefully, and, again, while Max considers this to be a function of the drummer, the keeper of the rhythm, the puncturing comes at rather an intricate point in the song. Leaving it to Hans Floral Anderson once more to run his guitar through an echo pedal and use his free hand to pick up the pin and prick the plastic. In the end, the balloons have to be overdubbed later and the whole track done anew as the levels go way red at every burst.

There are those who will tell you they can hear the influence of this tune yet again on a later film, as was par for the course with Cake Ass songs. This time foreseeing *Who's Harry Crumb?* Especially as Annie Potts herself was coming off the two heavily soundtracked movies of *Pretty In Pink* and *Jumpin' Jack Flash*. Though at this point the boys had only seen John Candy in *Stripes* and *The Blues Brothers*. This supposed psychic ability pertaining to future Hollywood hits could've perhaps made them millions. But they were clueless as to even its existence, let alone how to harness such power. Only history, years later, suggesting otherwise. For it seems to them they are borrowing titles *from* films rather than bestowing them down the eons. As seen on the following track The Most Wonderful Secret In The World, with Becca's heartmelting performance.

A most curious number closes out the album, and it's easy to see how people might interpret it as another nod to the long departed co-founder of the mighty Cake Ass. This reading of the song persists even for those who know that Blish brought in the original melodic idea. Shockingly, however, Hans Floral Anderson, going on about the tune in a letter to Cookie, failed to see the significance of its title, being so engrossed, as he was fond of repeating at the time, 'in the now'. But could Hans' claims that 38 Nightingale Road had been taken purely from the Tintin book *King Ottokar's Sceptre* really be true? In which on page six it is the address given of the KLOW restaurant serving Syldavian national cuisine. Or so *it* claims...

Cookie, having received his message three days earlier but only getting around to reading it when she finds herself with a free hour before she is due to meet some friends for drinks at a local roller rink, rings Hans straight away to get the scoop. It was so like Hans to leave out important details like the one she suspects. Phoning him first at his mother's place and then at Graph City, paying the long distance charges to ask if Hans Floral Nightingale is back in the band. And if so, have they become a quintet, and how does that work? A most unexpected monologue that leaves Hans Floral Anderson very confused on the other end of the line.

And to end the record like this? Was the restaurant wishful thinking? To anyone familiar with the source material, they'd know that the venue is more of a front than where one would go to actually procure some food. But was this song so called because they were bringing the cake of their sound out to the world to dig in? At least placing it on the menu so people could order it. Something that couldn't really be said of *Formaldehyde Hydro!*... Is 38 Nightingale Road then the ultimate Cake Ass mission statement? Hans Floral Anderson seemed to think so. Even with it set in the fictional foreign land of an old comic book. In his mind, were Buttery Cake Ass already huge in Syldavia? Which would not be such an enormous leap to Hungaria... But who among us can discern the hidden cartography of another's imagination?

The song, Reg informs us, is deceptively gentle. For halfway through, one can no longer ignore the sense of an eruption on the horizon, or rather the vanishing point below, coming as it feels from beneath one's feet. As would only be proper with the Hanses. If Reg Button's theory about how the tracks line up side by side is correct, no matter how unintentionally, then 38 Nightingale Road must correspond to 13th Florist, the two numbers songs, and is surely another, at least subliminal, ode to Hans Floral Nightingale, wherever his soul may be. And what was he doing on this occasion of his former band making one of history's great lost albums? For at the end of that one magical night, the album is deemed recorded. Done and dusted, and what is coming around the corner, what delights the mythical land of rock n roll stardom has awaiting them as they barrel headlong towards its gates, is anybody's guess...

PART FOUR - DEBUT(TERY) ALBUM

Live In Hungaria, Buttery Cake Ass' first full-length record, is completed just before the stroke of midnight. With both Cinderella *and* Smashing Pumpkins still aways away from slipping onto the world stages, this is the real deal, the primordial batter. Having to be back at work bright and early Monday morning, Reg 'Baton' Button, after some minor celebrations - for truth be told, they were all exhausted - grabbing maybe 27 winks under the pinball machine before hightailing it back to his and Blish's hometown. The plan is for him to come down the following weekend for any overdubs that might be necessary, namely Max's pinballing on Artchery, the balloon barrage of Crumbs, and to mix the thing, Walter not wanting the shop left too long in disarray.

Knowing they have something special, Buttery Cake Ass become terrified of anything happening to the tapes in the meantime. Suggestions for their protection ranging from burying them in the forest with an X marks the spot map - Hans all ready to go, sure he'd seen a shovel somewhere in his mother's garage - to taking out a safety deposit box in a local financial institution. But with their mindset being so Clash-oriented, the dubby strains of Bankrobber are never far away, speedily putting the ki-bosh to that suggestion. To the more literal minded, it may have made more sense to stash the tapes in a nearby bakery, miles from both bank and forest, with the discussion following that Davey Down had heard baking tapes actually restores them. But aside from the reels not yet needing any rehabilitation, Hans also has irrational childhood superstitions from old fairy tales about large ovens. They don't know anyone at said bakery either, so it would seem an odd request at best. And one that stood a good chance of being denied.

In the end, Walter keeps the tapes at his apartment, declining the band's offers to 'stand guard at his door in rotating shifts'. There are more important matters to attend to - figuring out how they are going to release the album, the live show plus other various promotions, and, perhaps even more pressingly, the cover art.

The annoying thing about this is that no one - well, at least our sources, Cookie and Reg Button - could really remember any details about the album sleeve. So here were Trig and I out searchin' for somethin' that we might not even recognize when we found it. Maybe we already had? I better not go down that road... But while its front cover is obscured in these viewers' memories, all (both) were certain the back was a photo of Blish Billings asleep underneath the pinball machine, shot late one night during the rehearsal stage. Nevermind that, to this day, neither Trig nor I have ever seen even an artist's rendering of Blish Billings. There can't be too many albums that depict a young man slumberin' away below any four-legged metal contraptions. So it will be doubly satisfyin' when we do find this, finally gettin' to see what this six-string magician looks like...and realizing that at long last it is *Live In Hungaria* we have in our hands! In this scenario, Trig and I are holdin' the record ourselves, not havin' someone point it out to us, or I daresay findin' it on the internet.

But as for that front cover - Woah, Nelly! Luckily, for us anyway, in that one letter Max did write to Cookie, he waxes on this too. Another letdown for the drummer was that the album didn't end up with the gatefold sleeve he had envisioned. Picturing as he was a scene involving the asteroid known as 434 Hungaria. Stumbling across this cool fact in recent months, not uncoincidentally he believes, with its discoverer also being named Max, and thus feels guided in his own quest to make the album. Steered not so much by the literal heavenly body, he is quick to clarify to Cookie, but rather the concept of Giant Rock. The numbers, along with his great love of Led Zeppelin's The Ocean, leading him to push the time signature of 7/4, as heard in sections of Artchery and Crumbs. Not that Buttery Cake Ass ever sounded anything like Led Zep. For Max, the sleeve should have displayed this asteroid on some sort of graph paper, paying homage to all Walter had done for them, but then when you opened the gatefold out, it becomes obvious that this satellite is simply the silver bullet in a giant galactic pinball game, hovering over the lycanthropic outline of the former Hapsburg Empire far below. 'Astro-Hungary', as Max had taken to referring to it.

Reg Button recalled the sleeve as being 'blue-ish'.

By the time Reg returns the following weekend to mix the album, he is armed with some potentially good news. Immediately greeting the group by asking Blish if he remembers Brouce Cozzins The Second. Blish replying in the affirmative, but then remembering what he remembered about this Brouce, putting forth the not unreasonable query - 'Why?'

Although he had since moved to the big city some twenty miles down the line, Brouce had gone to high school with Blish and Reg, and was still considered a daring sort of fellow around their hometown, which suited his musical tastes perfectly as The Human League were one of his favourite bands. There was also the rumor going around that Brouce's real name was in fact Brouce Cozzins Jr. and that he changed it to avoid people quoting the Van Halen song ...And The Cradle Will Rock at him, as he was self-conscious about having failed out of college. But men like Brouce don't have to worry about such formalities as degrees and the like when they have what is traditionally known as 'hutzpah'. Brouce was gonna do just fine in this world. And having recently come into possession of some $750, instead of using it to add to his already enormous record collection, thought he too might like to get in the game. Cozzins, coming from a large family who often had assorted business requiring him to bring his extra hands back to town, was now sitting at the local diner mulling these music industry aspirations over over a particularly salty slice of pickle dipped into a particularly vanilla vanilla milkshake when who should walk in with the news that he is recording an album with old Strings Stringfellow's new group than Reg 'Baton' Button himself.

The two get to talking, further about music of course, Brouce describing his current position as 'perched at the edge of the diving board, with the waters looking welcoming.' Though, never one to cautiously dip in a toe and test, his mind remained uncrossed as to the temperature or if there might be anything lurking beneath the waves to strip said toe to the bone. Reg, hip to the band's situation as well as Walter's feelings towards forking out for another record, keeping these elements close to his chest as he relays the details of his first real foray into music production. Brouce growing pretty excited over what he is hearing and feeling good enough about this prospect to even confess to Reg how he won that cool 7-50...

Having been upstate the previous week and happening upon a gathering of folks who had a bear in their sights. The party were tickled pink by the creature's movements and, as one does in those parts, money started being put on the line anticipating what said bear might do next. Culminating in the be-all end-all bet as to whether or not this animal might act out each semaphore of the Beatles' *Help* album cover over a 24 hour period. Everyone 'bug-eyed the F out' on Jolt cola and numerous coffee concoctions by the end of it. The judges deeming Fuzzy Wuzzy's motions in that final hour 'close enough', ordering folks to pay up. Brouce having gotten in on the action, taking up odds that were remarkably only 75 to 1.

Feeling, well, 'guilty' isn't exactly the word for it, but beyond reasonably rewarded that only ten dollars has brought him so much good fortune, Brouce believes it best to bestow these blessings on others. And bankrolling a Buttery Cake Ass album seems the very thing. Talk about a ticket to ride...

Reg returning bright and early that next Saturday morning and moving his gear back into place. Walter closing the shop that day so the boys can devote full concentration to their work. There's no way he can extend that time to the entire weekend due to the pressing needs of early Sunday morning archery enthusiasts, but one day should be enough to suffice.

It was Cookie who had mentioned Reg 'Baton' Button's name to us, giggling as she put his middle name in air quotes usin' all eight fingers. A name we earmarked for later use, of course. But it wasn't until a full two months after our return from the wilds of New York City's record emporiums that Trig arrived at my front door, bent double over wide spread knees tryin' to catch his breath, and holdin' one of the 12"s we had brought home in the trunk. 'Trig,' I asked, 'why didn't you just call me?' But as he removed the inner sleeve and lifted it up to my eyes, pointin' at the text in the lower right hand corner, I knew why he had run as fast as he could to my abode. For there, on Clown Damage's full-length debut, *Dig That Cat, He's Really Gone*, read the words 'Recorded by Reg 'Baton' Button at Superconductor Studios'. Could it really be he of whom Cookie spoke? How many Reg 'Baton' Buttons are there? It was back to the library telephone directories post-haste. We started with Seattle, Chicago, and Chapel Hill, usin' the best guesses of the time, and Humboldt County, simply because we were Thomas Pynchon fans. Superconductor Studios not appearin' in any of them. Even phonin' 411 directory services provided not a clue. But we kept at it, callin' record shops and venues in these greater metropolitan areas, speakin' with folks who might know peeps who might've heard somethin', eventually bein' given a number for such a locale on the outskirts of Portland, Oregon. How can we ever repay that gentle voice on the other end of the line at Disco Graffiti? If you're readin' this, know that we are eternally grateful. Reg was a hard man to get on the line, and we spent our time between attempts going through the rest of our record collections searchin' for anything else that might bear his stamp. Eventually turnin' up Heinkel Schneinkel's There Is A Pig...(Floating In My Passageway) 7" and The Loud Sounds *Sounding Loud* EP. When we finally did get a hold of Reg three weeks later, he was quite shocked to hear from us, but as he'd just completed work on the latest Cracked Tractor single and was kickin' back with a nice hot cup of lapsang souchong, he soon warmed to the hearth of memories we had set ablaze.

Reg tellin' Trig & I how pleasant the whole mixing experience was. For in years to come, as his career took off, he was no stranger to various acts of soul-challenging shenanigans. Rival bandmates anglin' to sneak in the studio and add or subtract tracks hopin' the other wouldn't notice. There was that one time some dude had him EQ'ing 45 seconds of rain sounds for five hours straight, and then tryin' to talk Reg into only payin' by the song. The following day that same dude's friend spillin' a can of cola on the mixing board and attemptin' to clean it up by lightin' it on fire. But back in these simpler days with Buttery Cake Ass it was all about simply showin' up and lettin' the thrill of creation lead you where it may.

On the ride down to Graph City, Reg had been thinking that someone taking a chance on a bear like that and it paying off might just be what Buttery Cake Ass needed. And now, after plugging everything in and setting up the spool of tape, explaining to the boys Brouce's situation. Though feeling it best to keep stumm about how he came across the money. Walter looking as relieved as the band are excited that someone else might want to release their record. Even if this Brouce guy hadn't yet heard it.

The early afternoon is spent on Max's thwarted attempts to lay down a new pinball track. Which, as mentioned previously, cannot seem to capture the energy of Hans' original take. But despite the overwhelming disappointment for the drummer, the record is sounding amazing. The balloons are nailed in one take. The vocals still fresh a week later, no overdubs needed there. All Reg's meticulous note-keeping means the mixing goes pretty quickly. And while Davey Down, Max, and Walter are out bringing back dinner, Hans and Blish staying behind with their baby, who should come knockin' on Graph City's door, just when the boys should require an extra pair of hands for some particularly tricky manipulation of the faders on Crumbs? Well, Byron Thebes himself, who had helped them design their lighting rig back when Hans Floral Nightingale was still in the band. Byron is back from college and, sensing something might be going on with the group, had headed down to ol' Graph City. His spider senses not leading him astray, now moving his digits where he is told. Once that mix is completed, Hans and co. playing him some of the album so far. Byron loving it, already picturing the abacus solos when they take things further out in the live show.

You'll remember Byron Thebes as previously being referred to as 'sometimes being referred to as 'The Fifth Buttery Cake Ass''. But now with the addition of Blish, and even Reg 'Baton' Button working wonders behind the board, anyone considering using such words would have to contemplate amending them to 'the Sixth or Seventh Buttery Cake Ass', even uttering this new phrase as a whole. For who truly knew how things stacked up in the grand order of Assland? An argument could be made for Walter taking a number too...

After a break for food, the final tunes are polished off and everyone is kicking back with the lights down low to hear the finished album all the way through. Byron happily joining in. And when Hans, casting a sideways check with Walter first, declares it a wrap, Reg starts running off a tape to bring back to Brouce and hopefully arrange a meeting, though no one can see any reason why anyone wouldn't want to release this astonishing record. Talk again turning to maybe getting it to some of the major labels, with Walter casually reminding them of the DIY spirit of the majority of their idols.

No one really wanting to leave this magical place where they heard *Live In Hungaria* in its entirety for the first time. Byron's excitement extending to the album title as well. And so everybody begins, well you wouldn't exactly call it 'celebrating', more like mulling around engrossed in celestial visions, but staying within Graph City's walls nonetheless until well after daybreak. Reg Baton again grabbing some sleep under the pinball machine in the early hours before packing up his car and heading home. But not before the boys ask him to do their live sound at an upcoming gig the following Thursday. Driving away right before the early Sunday morning archery crowd assails Graph City's front door, Reg now on a mission to get their tape released.

Unable to reach Brouce that first day back with the mix, Reg nevertheless managing to make a plan the following afternoon to meet up the next evening. Reg describing having the tape but not being able to share it being like 'that Buddhist parable about holding the hot coal in your hands...except in a good way...so maybe not like that at all...but still...kinda?...'

Meeting up at the diner again. Reg arrives to find Brouce already there, just sitting looking worried at the counter, stirring up another vanilla milkshake, this time with a long pretzel stick. It's the salt, ya know?

Reg sliding onto the seat next to him. Brouce not even glancing up, seeming to continue a diatribe started well earlier - 'What if it was asking for help...' - and clutching his fist tightly in anguish.

Reg taken aback for a minute before slowly realizing that Brouce might be talking about the bear. Leaving another minute to gauge the seriousness of the situation, before pointing out that the semaphore on The Beatles' *Help* album doesn't actually spell out 'help', but rather 'NUJV', or 'NVUJ' if you've got the American Capitol Records release, Brouce of course having both.

'Right,' Brouce counters, 'but what if the bear knew that?...And was trying to just cut to the chase, thinking everyone was a Beatles fan or why else would they go through all the trouble to make so many copies of such a photograph? It being a bear, not really understanding how the mass production of records works. Or I mean it could've really learned semaphore wrong, precisely from that album cover, and genuinely believed it was asking for help...'

Reg, again, trying to be the voice of reason. 'But you said it took almost 24 hours for the bear to make those gestures. Surely if it was in need of assistance, it would've communicated that more insistently than wandering around willy-nilly for a day and occasionally - I'm assuming accidentally - miming John, Paul, George, and Ringo?' Brouce cutting in, 'What if bears operate on a completely different time scale?'

Reg remaining calm. 'If it was asking for help, it could've done so in many other ways.'

Brouce straightening up. 'Ya know, ya might be right, Reg...' Slapping him on the back, 'Thanks buddy. So what's up, why d'ya want to meet?'

Reg raising an eyebrow. Brouce's excitement about the tape when he finally got him on the phone had been palpable. Uncertain now how to respond, Reg simply sliding the cassette case across the counter to him. Brouce's eyes widening in recognition, then casting them about the diner to see how they would play the thing. 'We're gonna listen to this? Why did we meet here?'

Reg, a most patient man, as recording engineers have to be, replying 'You told me to meet you here.'

Brouce standing up and signaling for Reg to follow as they head out to Brouce's car, a beat-up secondhand 1977 black Pontiac Firebird Trans Am. 'I used some of that money to put this new stereo in. Figure I can expense it. Glad I don't have to return it now to give the cash to some wildlife foundation for wayward bears. They went silent when I brought up the sign language. Though do ya think studying that bear might be important for science? Like how it might be nature's biggest Beatles fan?'

'Just put in the tape, Brouce...'

Mr. Cozzins the Second does as he is told. The Firebird idling in the parking lot as Brouce cranks up the volume. And like the Phoenix of his vehicle's name, Brouce's spirits rise from the ashes of self-pity as the mighty Artchery washes over them. 'What's the dinging sound?'

Reg smiling. 'Pinball machine.'

'F Yes!' Brouce pounding the steering wheel. 'Now that's what I call music' and cranks the volume even higher.

Although the plan had been to just sit in the parking lot and listen, the tunes carry the car out onto the road. Brouce taken with everything, especially Crumbs, with the balloons popping and the way it reconfigures the melody of Relics Of Forgotten Futures, spotting that right away. Then moisture coming to his eyes when Becca starts to sing on The Most Wonderful Secret In The World, exhaling 'she has the voice of a vanilla angel' and catching the salt of his tears on his tongue. Somehow picking up on the Frenchness and the bit about taking the I out of 'moist' as he waxes poetical comparing the tune to the film *How To Steal A Million*. Most likely mixing this up with *Roman Holiday*, the exquisite emotion of that final scene, even as he goes on about Hugh Griffith's eyebrows. Later, when Brouce would gush to Hans Floral Anderson about all this, it seemed evident to Hans that he understood The Floorist philosophy and was therefore the right man to release their record. With the tape rewinding to hear again, they pull back into the diner parking lot to grab some celebratory vanilla milkshakes with ultra-sturdy fries for dipping before heading back out

114

on the road.

Brouce, overjoyed at the prospect, asks at one point, 'I'm gonna release this?' Then looking a bit worried.

Reg calling him on it. 'What's up, Brouce? You do still have the money, right? You were all stoked to start your own record label...'

Brouce turning his head off to the side, pretending to be interested in something on the pavement. 'Yeah...Yeah, of course. It's gonna be great. I got the money...'

Reg knowing what's coming next. After a moment's pause, 'Well...maybe not all of it...but no, we're definitely gonna put this out.' Reg raising his own not insignificant brow at that 'we'.

Over the next few days Brouce Cozzins II works himself further and further into a tizzy over what to call his new label. Thinking it should be some sort of tribute to the bear who gave him the idea and the money to do this in the first place. Even despite some of that cash now being gone. Thinking maybe Aquarius Records and explaining his reasoning to Reg, who has by now, by virtue of having recorded the album Brouce is planning on putting out, become his somewhat unwilling confidant. 'Ya know how Aquarius is the water *bear*er? And the bear did perform the semaphore for J next to a stream...'

Reg patiently putting it that perhaps this would not be obvious to everyone who hears the name.

Brouce bouncing back with 'Of course, of course... But it would also be a nod to one of my favourite mail order catalogues. That shop in San Francisco, ya know? I just ordered a stack a records from them the other day...'

Soon seeing that he hasn't won Reg's approval, Brouce tries a different tack. 'How about naming it after a famous bear? Like Paddington, Rupert, Yogi, Pooh-'

Reg stopping him. 'You *can't* call your label Pooh Records if the band you're going to release is named Buttery Cake Ass...'

Brouce conceding the point, but not without a grimace.

Reg reflecting to Trig and I that he was quite green back then, mistakenly believin' this was the sort of stuff you had to put up with in the music industry to get things done. And in many ways it was. But you can move on from that, he was sure to advise us, confidin' also that he wished he had thought of The Jungle Book at the time as Baloo Records has a cool ring to it, especially if you're doing coloured vinyl, and Brouce would've liked the allusion to Crumbs.

Reg *did* suggest using the word Ursine. Brouce's blank face prompting him further. 'It means bear-like...maybe Ursa Major Records...or Ursa

116

Minor...the Little Dipper...' But Brouce taking 'ursine' and rolling it around on his tongue, wondering aloud, 'How about Cosine? But pronounce it more like Cozzins...Cozine...' Reg hoping this isn't indicative of any future loans needing to be procured. But then, as if there had been an echo, Brouce picking up on what Reg had said a minute ago. 'Big Dipper Records...Big Dippre Cords...have it the way the English spell 'centre' and like 'theatre', ya know with the E and R reversed...so it would be pronounced 'Dipper' but it would be spelt Big Dip Re Cords...'

Reg stony-faced. Soon thinking it best to steer Brouce back to the sound of his self. 'Second Records has a certain charm to it?' Brouce eagerly following him back to the Cozzins theme. But Reg can't seem to convince Brouce that just because a word is sometimes used in conjunction with 'cousins' doesn't mean it will automatically imply this to the masses. Kissing Records doesn't give off the proper vibe. Distant Records has something to it and is put on the backburner. Reg speaking with wonder now to Trig & I. 'We even did an anagram of 'cousins' and came up with Sonic U. Imagine if we had used that? I mean this was 1983!'

Finally, days later, settling on Removed Records. With regards to the availability of the first album Brouce would be releasing, oh how appropriate this would turn out to be...

On the evening the label name is decided upon, Reg also receives a call from a very hesitant Blish Billings, put up to the task by his fellow Cake Assers asking about that dude who potentially wants to put out their record. It so happening that Brouce is over at Reg's place, showing him logo designs, and getting even more excited, grabbing the phone and telling Blish about choosing Removed.

And so the following weekend Reg and Brouce are headed to Graph City to meet the band, blasting *Live In Hungaria* the whole way down in the Firebird. Reg still excited to be listening to this, his first major production. The mood only slightly deflated by his concern over the moustache beginning to appear on Brouce's upper lip. Sure, it goes with the car but Reg is hoping it isn't a sign that Brouce might be hiding something. He convinces himself to put it out of his mind as the rest of Brouce's demeanor is rather open. As is his style of dress, for that matter. The first jams shorts Reg has ever seen, shirt more unbuttoned than not, and no socks. Reg doesn't know how one can drive without socks, again banishing this from his thoughts as he hopes for the best from this meeting between musicians and mogul-in-the-making.

Parking the Firebird - another car that could not haul much equipment - right out front and strolling into the record store. 'Strings!' Brouce beams, holding out his hand to shake. The guitarist moving forward to greet and correct him. 'Blish' he replies.

Brouce screwing up his face, correcting *him* - '*Brouce*' - and looking hurt that the former Hubert 'Strings' Stringfellow doesn't remember his name. Blish smiling, 'Naw man, they call me Blish now. Blish Billings. It's good.'

Brouce recovering himself, 'Well yeah it is!' Smacking Blish on the shoulder and walking in to meet the gang, his excitement back up now, gravitating naturally to Hans Floral Anderson, whose distinction as leader is obvious. Davey Down and Max Beta crowding in, all the boys somewhat in awe of this man who might actually want to pay money to release *Live In Hungaria*.

Upon being introduced to Walter, Brouce reaches into his pocket in order to pump the record store man's hand with three fifty dollar bills. 'Pleasure to meet ya, I hope this covers the expenses.' Walter not really sure what to say but accepting the cash readily, mentally ticking off the costs incurred so far - food, gas money for Reg, loss of revenue from closing the shop, maybe wear and tear on the pinball machine... Hans and Brouce getting along like wildfire. Brouce knowing how to handle artists and their egos but also greatly impressed by Hans' immense talent but relaxed manner. Three-quarters of an hour of conversation later, with Brouce on his second round of going through Graph City's racks, continuously adding to an imposingly large stack of records on the counter that Walter hopes he is planning to buy, they send out for more cheeseless pizzas and more or less get down to business.

Davey Down blurting, 'Yeah, Reg told us you won $750...'

Brouce, who is continuing to browse, sidles up to the counter, placing some more 12"s on the pile. 'Yeah, about that, I was thinkin' we start small. Press 300 copies, see how that fares. Then we take it from there. I love first pressings, man, we'll make that one special. Give it some identifying marks so it can always be spotted as one of the originals...' Slapping Davey Down on the back before returning his attention to the Rock Various Artists divider.

Reg realizing what the band isn't. That Brouce has already spent a significant portion of that $750, leaving him with about $300 to press the album. Reg wondering what part of the math included the $150 he is now dropping on records from Graph City, and of course the other $150 he seemed to think licensed him the rights from Walter.

Hans flipping thru Brouce's pile which reveals itself to be punctuated by albums like Edward Bear's self-titled 1972 release, Aerosmith's *Toys In The Attic*, *Barclay James Harvest And Other Short Stories*, which also came out in '72 and has the song Ursula on it, the Sugar Bear LP from 1970, Elvis' Teddy Bear single in the 7"s sitting atop the serious stack of full-lengths... Hans considering the resonance between these titles somewhat peculiar. Brouce himself explaining to Reg on the drive back that night that it seemed to be a sign that there were so many bear records at Graph City.

Reg feeling roped in now, like Brouce's unpaid personal secretary,

120

setting up meetings with the Cake Ass, whom he really doesn't know much better than Brouce does. And although the band had had the artwork ready to go at that first rendezvous, they didn't want to scare off a potential backer by appearing too eager. However, at the next visit, when they present their design ideas to Brouce is when he instigates the name change from Buttery PIAS to A Real Fridge In Real Life. Continuing to accumulate quite the heap of another to-buy pile on Graph City's counter, Brouce is bouncing around the store pointing out what he alone hears as overtones of Magazine in the tune, telling them how he loves the concept of The Cure's transmutational refrigerator and that this could then extend to reference that first Buzzcocks album, *Another Music In A Different Kitchen*... After putting forth his thoughts about this not being their theme song and thus requiring an appellative adjustment, he pauses in front of where Walter keeps the soda pop. His mind kicking into overdrive, aswirl with the possibilities of what might happen to other acts should they enter such an appliance. Then uttering 'Imagine if it was a real fridge in real life...' All look at each other, eyebrows raised. Brouce had not intended to find a solution so quickly, but there it is. He feels he's in the game now, and sets about changing the track list on the mock-up sleeve with a crafting knife. The rest of the tunes he loves the titles for. And so with everything named like in the second book of Genesis, but not sounding like any incarnation of Phil Collins & co., Buttery Cake Ass has album and art both ready to go, passing them off to Brouce Cozzins whose excitement, though a little unbalanced, is also contagious.

A month goes by without them hearing even a word back from Brouce. Assuaging their fears is the knowledge that their would-be financier is irritating the hell out of Reg 'Baton' Button with his myriad questions on how to do just about anything related to running a record label. The rest of the group getting this from Blish, who is starting to collaborate with the engineer on some music, Reg calling Blish in on some sessions he is running back in their hometown, picking him up a few times a week to lay down some of his signature blistering guitar work. When Brouce finally does get in touch again, it is about the pressing matter of what to write in the run-out groove of the vinyl.

Brouce being keen on the phrase Semaphore Bears No Resemblance. A nod to, but perhaps also a cry *for*, *Help*. He is still smarting from the record plant telling him they can't fit an etching of the California state flag in the deadwax on either side. With its picture of a grizzly and the fact that Bear California can be abbreviated as BCA, Brouce has embraced this as 'beyond perfect'. Even despite their physical distance from The Golden State. He hasn't told the band yet, but reflected in those initials he also sees himself, in that Brouce Cozzins The Second can also be read as Brouce Cozzins Again.

And speaking of the word 'again', some were thinking that the ideal etching for the run-out groove on side two would be the full spelling out of PIAS - Play It Again Sam. If *Casablanca* hadn't had the balls to say it, they would. An instruction to everyone, whether they are called Sam or not, to flip the record over and repeat the listening experience. But Brouce, as he was known to do, quibbling over the finer points, that perhaps it should read Play It Again Sam Even If Your Name's Not Sam, and then worrying that if the pressing plant messed up and printed this on the A-side, people following the instructions would never get to hear the whole album, leaving his personal favourite, Crumbs, unheard by the masses.

Max Beta weighing in on the topic at hand. At long last over his wounded pride enough to speak about his feelings, interjecting 'But Real Fridge, what we called PIAS, is *on* side one. We could have a P-I-A-S for both? Like the first side could read Pinball Is A Scene...or Pinball Is A Science...or - ', getting more excited now, remembering his plans for the cover art, 'Pinball Is All Space.'

Brouce, unwilling to let his original idea go, though warming to Max's suggestion. 'Or Pinball Is A Semaphore comma Bears No Resemblance...'

Hans Floral Anderson clearing his throat. 'Actually I was thinking we could use that old phrase of Hans'...' Everyone going quiet now, for it is a rare occasion indeed that Hans Floral Nightingale's name is invoked. Brouce, none the wiser, thinking Hans Floral Anderson is referring to himself in the third person, and is on board with this bold move for an unknown artist. A pregnant pause as no one is precisely sure which phrase Hans means, and half the listeners never having met the man. Hans looking each of them in the eye, nodding as he reaches Max, Davey Down, and Walter. 'An embalmed gecko doesn't change colors...'

All, slowly, indicate their approval.

Brouce keeping silent for the moment, pausing to scratch his upper lip while quietly registering that his bear on one side and a gecko on the other would be an incredibly powerful statement, perhaps enough to make this record unstoppable. Later that evening suggesting that with his plan to have each pressing of the record distinct from the others, over time they can etch in every one of these most excellent phrases, and the first round of 300 should sell out quick as look-at-ya.

Reg couldn't actually remember what they ended up using for the run-out grooves. I know, I know. Trig and I were crushed too. But to be fair, the man was givin' us an incredible amount of information and, as he told us, he was surprised he even recalled this much. *Live In Hungaria* having been the first of several hundred records that he's been involved with since. And if one of these etchings *was* 'an embalmed gecko doesn't change colors', it would certainly lend more credence to the theory that those ending songs were some sort of tribute to Hans Floral Nightingale.

Despite the excitement-tinged worry about their album not appearing immediately before their eyes now that they'd recorded it, Buttery Cake Ass now have other pressing concerns. That gig to prepare for, and a rehearsal space to find, as Walter has already put the shop back in order. All recognizing that he has been more than kind to them, a man of true nobility, but they are sad indeed to no longer be using Graph City as Buttery Cake Ass HQ. Being as it had been the site of so much intense focus and creativity, the band seeming to live there, Blish literally doing so, as they made the record. The problem is where to go. Even if Hans wanted to head back to his mother's garage, she'd recently cleaned it out, renting it as a one bedroom apartment to a traveling gourmet cheese salesman. A real slap in the face to Hans' dairy-free lifestyle. Byron Thebes coming to the rescue again, in his continuing capacity of turning the lights on for the band.

Though in this case it gets complicated with all sorts of shadows. Byron himself having found digs in a disused light bulb manufacturing building. Abandoned years before, Byron discovering that its office still has one working outlet, one he won't question, and so takes it over as his bedroom. Soon considering that the ground floor below would make a great space to play music in. Buttery Cake Ass would only have to score a generator of some sort, keeping stumm about his own source of electricity lest he somehow jinx it. It's a big enough area, they could treat it like a venue, maybe even one day turn it into one. Put a stage in, a booth in the back for sound and lights, construct a skate ramp or two... Best of all, until anyone says anything - and full of the invincibility of youth, they expect this to last forever - it would be free.

The boys suspicious about what might happen to their equipment if left overnight. Byron, who is a bit more freewheeling, unconcerned about such matters his two weeks thus far in the place, suggesting buying a couple of padlocks for the doors, as long as they give him a key. And thus Buttery Cake Ass starts preparing for their next live outing, and their first proper one with Blish. An actual show being markedly different from playing in the same store as ardent archery enthusiasts on the make, no matter how many times they did it, dozens as it had been... The performance on the horizon happens to again be at the bowling alley where they were mislabelled as simply 'Candy Aardvarks', so it goes without saying there is a lot to prove.

The only part of the album artwork still in abeyance has been the BCA logo itself. And now with it being vital that the denizens of this particular bowling alley get their name right, Hans finds it imperative to strip away all the fluff that has again begun to accumulate since Hans Floral Nightingale's departure, and keep the show flyer as simple as possible. And in doing so, happens upon a minor miracle. Perfectly in tune with how good, how 'right now', the band is sounding, he finds that just by lining up each word of their name one above the other, the final row from top to bottom spells out 'YES'.

BUTTERY

CAKE

ASS

Brouce driving Reg down to do the sound. It taking some convincing to get the promoter to give the group any sort of guest list. Byron walking in with the Cake Asses and Walter. The kid running the night wasn't gonna ask the older gentlemen for money as Walter sets up a merch booth consisting of 30 odd copies of *Formaldehyde Hydro!*, some BCA patches Davey Down has fashioned out of old boxer shorts - which, thankfully, no one buys - and two crates of Graph City stock.

Upon accepting the gig, the band had begun to rehearse playing the album from start to finish in order, interspersed with little snippets of music they have been working on to connect the songs, interludes that imply space travel between the planets of the pieces. Walter, catching sight of the set list and noticing that neither song from the 7" he released is on there, has a word with his protégés. 'I get that you're excited about playing your new material, but you also have a record that is already out, and in order for people to know about that, you should be playing at least one of the songs on it.' Too gracious to mention that he is nowhere near recouping what he paid to put out *Formaldehyde Hydro!* The band of course listening attentively whenever Walter speaks. Only that Blish has never played either song before. So, spying a turntable in the bowling alley office, the boys bribe a young member of staff with a 7" to let them in so Blish can sit with his guitar and learn the title track. The youthful employee thinking this is so cool, assuming that because he's never heard of them, not knowing much about music himself, Buttery Cake Ass must be this hugely popular act touring America and needing private quarters in which to conduct important business. Hans, Davey Down, and Max Beta smiling excitedly at the new lines to the chord progression Blish is firing off as they crowd into the room under the pretext of seeing if the new guy needs any help deciphering the sections, when in reality each musician's memory requires a certain amount of jogging. The promoter soon knocking on the door to tell them they're on at 9 sharp and they've got 45 minutes because he's feeling generous.

Skulking out of the office, abuzz with that peculiar mixture of nervousness and excitement whose home is the pre-show air, at not only getting to play their new album live while unleashing Blish Billings onto the world, there is now also the wild card of Formaldehyde Hydro thrown into the works. An early mission statement whose power they sense Blish is going to harness into thunderbolts to discharge at the crowd via his six electric strings. And while the band are awash with such complicated emotions, Hans spies Becca walk in, accompanied by her friends Cynthia and Angelina, neither of whom he has seen since high school. So stunned he greets them with the words 'Are you here to bowl?'

Becca laughs, 'We're here to see you, silly...I love the tape you gave me.' The frontman having left a cassette of *Live In Hungaria* in her mailbox a week ago.

Hans not knowing how to respond, stares down at his hands for a moment before the idea strikes him, 'You should join us...for your song.'

'Yeah?' Becca queries, a mixture of nerves and excitement herself.

'Yeah,' Hans replies.

And so back into the office they all march to rehearse The Most Wonderful Secret In The World. Max drumming on the small beat-up orange couch across from where Hans and Becca are perched on the manager's desk, his sticks occasionally catching on one of the many cigarette burn holes pockmarking the upholstery. Cynthia and Angelina heading to the bar, to be joined ten minutes later by an even more jittery version of the now extended band. Hans, cheeks rosy with embarrassment, looking slightly to Becca's left, 'I would've asked you earlier but I didn't think you'd wanna come.' She rolling her eyes and playfully pushing him on the shoulder.

The boys take the stage at exactly 9 o'clock. The three young ladies making up a third of the crowd, an entity that will grow noticeably smaller when Becca hops on stage to sing. Cake Ass launching wordlessly into Artchery. Brouce getting so excited he starts punching Walter in the bicep, singing the missing pinball parts into his ear.

Brouce has been told about the little interstitial interludes that would punctuate the set, but when Hans starts singing the third number - where they have strategically placed Formaldehyde Hydro to disguise the fact that they don't really know it - he turns to Walter to ask what this new song is. Walter responding by holding up the 7" and Brouce immediately reaches into his pocket to give the Graph City man more cash. 'More' because during the first act he has already purchased a healthy stack of vinyl from Walter's crates.

As the post-13th Floorist interlude, what would later be known as Bronze, begins to wind down, the house soundman scuttles past Reg and Byron to grab the monitor mic and announce 'One more'. A most unexpected statement causing much befuddlement - the band has been onstage for 40 minutes and only gotten through half of the album.

After wasting a minute thirty of their remaining five standing around confused, Hans stepping forlornly to the mic, glancing towards Becca with an apologetic shrug and announcing 'This is our last one', before slipping into Relics Of Forgotten Futures, the continuity of their original sonic plan having been shattered by that most unwelcome intrusion into their monitors. Brouce's confusion slipping to annoyance and disappointment as it dawns on him that they won't be performing his Crumbs this evening. He had been looking forward to hearing the song live for days now, talking Reg's ear off about it on the car ride down.

The house staff flashing the lights at 9:45, so insistently that 30 seconds later Cake Ass have to cut two and a half minutes from Relics, scurrying to get their gear off stage. Then, as the headliners head on, slinking out to the parking lot to discuss the situation, though at first too baffled to speak. Brouce soon barging out to address things directly. 'What happened?!'

Shrugs and uncertain glances are not an answer but they are all that is forthcoming.

Max Beta, tapping his foot on the pavement, ever the keeper of time, soon pointing out what no one has yet really realized. 'Guys, I think the album is longer than 45 minutes.'

Before this has time to sink in, Becca, Cynthia, and Angelina push through the doors outside, and Hans begins to apologize profusely. The rest of the band and crew silently pondering the future. Blish going over his performance in his head in a manner that can't be expressed in words anyway. Brouce stepping forward to propose the grand solution that has just entered his mind. 'We'll do a live album then...*Live In Hungaria...Live*...it'll be epic!'

The mass introspection ceases as everyone turns to look Brouce's way, his face illuminated by a nearby streetlamp, and despite the fact that *Live In Hungaria* itself is not yet even at the pressing plant, all quickly warm to this idea. 'Yeah, we can record the interludes...' 'Should we keep Formaldehyde Hydro in?...like as a bonus track?'...and other relevant and not-so considerations.

The promoter soon coming out to inform them that if they want to get paid, they are gonna have to watch some of the final band, it being 'only polite', and so the amorphous blob of Cake Ass connections makes its way back into the venue, now tripling the crowd size. Blish and Hans going up to Walter to get his opinion on things. In a good mood from having sold so many records, mostly to Brouce, Walter is enthusiastic. Blish asking for his thoughts on Formaldehyde Hydro which Walter had rated as a particularly good version, complimenting the guitarist on its new supplemental twists. Now telling Hans he should announce that they have the 7" for people to buy at the merch booth. Hans asking how many copies they sold and Walter just shaking his head.

Even though the promoter only, perhaps understandably, gives them $5 in the end, now that they have the goal of another album to work towards, all are in the mood to celebrate and thus adjourn to the diner, Brouce saying it will be his treat. Hans asking Becca and her friends to join them, the ten of them taking over two tight booths. Walter, being a sort of elder statesman, heading home. Brouce holding court about his grand plans for the band as he dips a variety of salty foodstuffs into a succession of large vanilla milkshakes, playing up musical connections Reg was doubtful he had. Cool as it would be for the Cake Ass to bag an opening spot on Hermes Triangle's next US tour, Reg has no idea how Brouce might manage such a thing. The conversations soon splintering off across the tables. Reg and Byron trading suggestions on how they could enliven the show for next time, Brouce and Max Beta enthusing over vintage pinball machines, throwing out the thought of filming a gig or two, maybe even making a video for MTV - 'How rad would it be if we were playing inside a pinball machine?' - Davey Down, Cynthia, and Angelina awkwardly looking around for some minutes before Angelina asking what they thought of the latest episode of *Family Ties* and each then enthusing over their favourite Alex and

Mallory moments, while Hans and Becca nestle each against the window across from the other, discussing the possibility of maybe making more music together. Hans was now writing some songs that he wasn't sure were appropriate for the band and Becca, to his delight, mentions that she has some poems she has been thinking about setting to music. Cookie told us how cute this all was as she received letters from each of them the following week. Clearly not wanting to admit the feelings that were blossoming, but both nevertheless detailing how Hans had asked if Becca needed a ride home as the group walked back to the parking lot even as she was pulling out her keys and Cynthia and Angelina were blatantly moving towards the passenger doors of Becca's car. And then offering him one. Only to, when they pull up in front of Hans' mother's house, have him remember that he was supposed to be at the rehearsal space to help the rest of the band unload the equipment. All three young women stifling giggles for the entirety of the subsequent ride out to this further destination.

Not paying rent has left Byron with money to burn on excesses such as ordering three slices of pumpkin pie to go as they leave the diner, excited to have them for lunch and dinner desserts the following day. But getting out of the car when he is first to return to the old light bulb factory, the top one spills off the other two to crash at his feet. His hands full, Byron opts to just leave it splattered on the pavement. And some might point to Hans Floral Anderson then slipping on this very slice of pumpkin pie when he eventually emerges from Becca's car as the beginning of the end of Buttery Cake Ass. The whole cake/pie dichotomy still a real consideration for this unsuspecting band.

PART FIVE - BUTTERY CAKE ASS COMES ALIVE!

Much like Fred from Goose Train would later do, Brouce Cozzins The Second has been positively buzzing over the *Formaldehyde Hydro!* 7", causing him to immerse himself deeper in the plans to record and release *Live In Hungaria Live*, stoked that it will include the frenzied new version of the 7"'s title track that he'd heard the other night with Blish taking the reins. Brouce envisioning a double LP, which in his more practical moments he spends some time considering how he can afford. Then wondering what other bear antics he might be able to bet on with any surety, practicality often being a dazzlingly coloured kite in galeforce winds to Brouce. He loves the double KISS *Alive!* records, especially with the kids holding the KISS banner on the back of the first one. Could he win enough money to fly the band to Cobo Hall in Detroit where that photo was taken, getting enough extras down to pack the place? Or maybe just bring a Buttery Cake Ass banner for a sneaky shot the next time KISS plays nearby? The arena would already be full... He hopes the crowds will grow accordingly for Buttery Cake Ass now that they have a series of live dates to dig their heels into, though the prospects the other night do not bode well.

Hans Floral Anderson, as Cookie has previously informed us, had never had a girlfriend before in his life. And to Cookie's amazement, manages to play it cool when Becca calls him the following day to see if he is ok, his slip in the pumpkin pie looking particularly bad from her vantage point inside the car. Though not enough to stop those once-stifled giggles from letting fly as soon as she started driving away.

Perhaps Hans didn't metaphorically slip in pumpkin pie again over the phone because *everything* is seeming so odd to him at this point in time. Brouce Cozzins, who is supposed to be putting out their first record, keeps phoning him or driving down to Graph City, buying piles of albums including more copies of *Formaldehyde Hydro!*, which of course being sales of a record that has not much met that fate, Walter isn't going to question. Often waiting around the shop to show Hans his album sleeve designs for *Live In Hungaria Live*, a record that doesn't actually exist yet but is based on one that very much does, one that Hans is dying to get out there. Brouce isn't much of an artist, as is apparent from his own sketches of the *Live In Hungaria Live* layout, but he soon has the foresight to hire local illustrators to get his visions down on the page. It must be said, some of them looked incredibly cool, endearing Max Beta to him by running with the drummer's intergalactic pinball machine idea and adding giant exotic interplanetary princesses and panthers to the scheme, derivative of, but making it now also rival, Hawkwind's *Space Ritual* for sheer awesomeness. Reg Baton constantly wondering, to himself so as not to alarm the band, where Brouce is getting the money for all this? And if he has it, why isn't he pressing the album that is already in his hands?

Then one day Reg gets a surprise call from Brouce, which isn't that unusual but its contents are. Brouce has finally been in touch with a pressing plant and wants to check with Reg about this 'mastering process' the dude had told him about and if it is either a) a step that could be avoided, or b) one Reg could do for considerably less than the plant was asking, ideally for free. Reg explaining that mastering is the dark art of readying a record for replication and one he wouldn't want to mess with, but that everything the guy at the plant told him seems perfectly reasonable. Brouce slurps in reply, nervously sucking down a homemade vanilla milkshake haphazardly mixed in the blender as he was dialing Reg's number, then crunching down on some potato chips, obvious even on the other end of the line by the crinkle of the bag. If they had been in the room together, Reg would've seen him also using the chips as a scoop for more of the shake, missing a good third of the time due to nerves and then using another chip to try and scrape the spillage out of his goatee and into his mouth. But being in the same location as Brouce Cozzins is something Reg 'Baton' Button is extremely glad to be avoiding at this juncture.

Meanwhile Cake Ass keep lining up gigs and rehearsing, getting the interstitial pieces tight and blasting Formaldehyde Hydro off to heights well beyond anyone's imagination from hearing the 7". 38 Nightingale Road also metamorphosizing into a juggernaut itself, of necessity with

136

it being the album closer and thus the last song they will play for the live record. Brouce starting to speak of it as *Live In Hungaria Live*'s Let Me Go, Rock N Roll, though there are no similarities whatsoever between the two songs.

On the third afternoon of Hans and Becca getting together to play music, progress is made on a different front. There has been no official 'date' as of yet - Hans having been preoccupied by what to do with 38 Nightingale Road, the importance of getting this right as the closing number a topic of much discussion the night before at Cake Ass practice. Brouce even popping in at the beginning, nodding along to their pronouncements and occasionally interjecting 'of course, of course'. But now, alone with Becca in her bedroom, acoustic guitar cradled in his hands, Hans starts to strum the opening strains of this tune, and Becca knowing it from the tape he had given her, begins to sing. Hans loves her voice, as well as the act of joining it for harmonies, and it is now that he sees something of the songbird in the titular creature, something he never had before with his old bandmate Hans Floral Nightingale. After a lovely rendition of the tune, and one that Hans secretly wishes would be the version to close out the new live album - and why not? Becca would already be on stage for The Most Wonderful Secret In The World, though he daren't suggest this idea so prematurely - the two get to discussing what they should call this new project of theirs. If indeed there is a 'project' to speak of... The song title appeals, but not so much 'Road', perhaps Court, or Nightingale Crescent? For this is another street altogether, leading off from the group, an avenue for only their two...

The night before, however, Max Beta had still been trying to work out what song Buttery Cake Ass should be shooting a video for. Something he and Brouce had spent a lot of time and milkshakes on in the hours leading up to rehearsal. While Artchery is arguably the most exciting tune on the record - and there is a particular thrill about thinking themselves the first group to be attempting to get a 12-minute video on MTV, clearly delineating Michael Jackson as a solo artist as opposed to band, and anyway theirs is a full 12 minutes of music with no dramatic breaks - this also proves to be a strategic problem. Not having an 'in' anywhere at the station, they would be approaching MTV cold with plans for an epic video, Michael Jackson at least having Epic Records behind him. In this rare instance Brouce Cozzins II doubting whether even he has the hutzpah for such a venture. Exploring their different options amounts to debating what other song from the record would be best represented by filling a pinball machine full of milk. Still, two years afterwards, the boys - and almost everyone they know, really - thinking the snare drum full of the stuff from the J. Geils Band Centerfold clip is the coolest thing they've ever seen. Well, after *Star Wars*... And fusing these two cinematic masterpieces together along with their favourite arcade game would have to be a winning combination. Disappointingly, there are preventative considerations here too, namely being able to afford to buy a pinball machine as whatever one they use will surely be destroyed by filling it with any form of liquid, let alone one with a white opacity. Doubting they could clean the machine as well as would be required to get their full deposit back. There is also the question of what a pinball machine full of milk would look like on film... The band's dairy-free lifestyle had to be taken into account as well, something Brouce Cozzins could never hold truck with, though he had been known to suck down a soy shake every now and again. Walter, catching wind of their plans, promptly moves the beverage fridge behind the front counter, well away from Graph City's own arcade game.

The next date is actually a big deal, their most high profile gig yet. Brouce making the arrangements and thereby banishing some of the doubts that have been growing in the group's mind. Glucose Maman are passing through the area and Brouce knows the guy setting up the show, using his charm and hutzpah to get Buttery Cake Ass on the bill. Walter is impressed as he's sold quite a few copies of Glucose Maman's debut 7"- *Man In A Dark Suit*. A tune in which only that title is repeated over three chords - to be fair, of a wide dynamic range - for three and a half minutes. He also loves their adamance in interviews that although yes, 'maman' is the French word for 'mom' and in that tongue the last consonant is silent, they themselves pronounce the N at the end. 'Sounds like it's spelt', they insisted. 'And not the wheat.'

Although Buttery Cake Ass are wired for the gig, the bright lights are not as luminous as they at first appeared. They would only be given a half-hour set time. Perfectly normal for an opening act, but not for a band intent on soon recording the double *Live In Hungaria Live* album. How would they ever get a chance to rehearse it all the way through? Strategies are thrown back and forth as neither side of the album will fit into thirty minutes with the interstitial jams they have now added in between. Formaldehyde Hydro too wanting a few more outings to firm it up. And it seems inconceivable not to open with Artchery, which would take up almost half their set. Blish putting it out there that they could simply extend Artchery to comprise the entire 30, and everyone is keen on this idea. Though what ends up written on the set list is Artchery, Formaldehyde, Relics, Indigo, and Crumbs. Brouce insisting his favourite tune be played this time, especially since he has set the whole thing up. Indigo being the connection between Crumbs and its predecessor, convenient in that it is also currently one of the shortest of these new pieces. All agreeing this new set list should do the trick. If Formaldehyde is performed at the frenetic speed they've been playing it at lately and there is no talking in between songs, just going straight into the next one, they'll come in a few seconds under the half hour.

In the end it was as thrilling as it sounds. Glucose Maman even wandering out into the crowd to watch them halfway through. Something they wouldn't have initially planned on doing after meeting Brouce Cozzins and listening to him expound on how great the record is, 'primarily Crumbs which they'll be playing tonight'. Brouce holding his breath for a minute when it starts, hoping it will be as good as he has been bragging. The Maman's boys, impressed, invite Blish to join them on guitar for the encore of Man In A Dark Suit and the other three to take backing vocals. An event Walter wished he had a tape recorder for, it seeming to make the whole putting out the 7" that nobody bought ordeal worthwhile. Brouce continuing to remedy this by purchasing four further copies, one for each member of Glucose Maman, who are delighted to receive them. Driving off in their van, waving the vinyl, and promising the Cake Asses they'll be on the bill the next time GM rolls through town. The band retiring to the diner, Walter joining them this time, caught up as he was in all the excitement. Becca and Hans resuming their places against the window, him beaming with pride and her reflecting that back to him. Cynthia and Angelina coming along as well, squeezing in either side of Davey Down, and everyone enthusing over how nice it was to play for an actual audience. That people they didn't know applauded their songs. And nervous as they had been, it turned out to be a very enjoyable experience.

The next gig however doesn't go nearly as well. Davey Down has booked them into a bar near their new practice space. The set originally prescribed as Artchery, Formaldehyde, A Real Fridge In Real Life, Periwinkle, and closing with The Most Wonderful Secret In The World. But when they arrive and see how rough the crowd is - locals who feel live music only interferes with their drinking time and thus get straight to pelting the opening band with half-full beer bottles - Hans doesn't want his and Becca's beautiful duet to meet a similar fate and have something that has grown so precious to him be tarnished. Barely at the holding hands stage of what seems like the blossom of a full-on relationship, if only Hans would get his act together to make it so, they have their first fight. Becca coolly replying that she hasn't rehearsed for weeks only to have them back out of it now, that she is a big girl and can take it. But the band, who are now uncertain about playing at all, agree with Hans that Most Wonderful Secret would be lost on this particular clientele, and so cut Periwinkle short to shift once again into Crumbs, delighting Brouce Cozzins of course. Becca brooding near the back of the venue with her friends who have come out to support her. Each one of whom considering the whisky glass Hans takes to the face during the closing number to be adequate payback for cutting her song.

There is no diner afterwards. Hans heading home alone to spend the rest of the disappointing evening with an ice pack over his cheek. Walter had turned around as soon as he walked in, not wanting to subject his records to any would-be violence or theft. Formaldehyde Hydro was kept in the set anyways, for they had grown rather fond of the song, and in truth it was the only thing that subdued the crowd that night.

Things have a way of working out though and the next show proves to be the proper place and time for Most Wonderful Secret's live debut. A local festival two towns over on the center green. Buttery Cake Ass, used to four enclosed walls, grumbling, but Brouce, who again has set up the gig, insists it will get them heard by a wider audience. Plus, they are given 45 minutes. This still being a few shy of allowing them to play the album in its entirety, they cut Relics and the songs with the numbers in the titles, opting to take The Most tunes out for a spin, as well as airing all the connecting colours in order. Well, the order they would play them in if they played the whole album straight through.

Artchery, Sepia, A Real Fridge In Real Life, Butterscotch, The Most Scathingly Brilliant Idea, Chartreuse, Bronze, Indigo, Crumbs,

Fuchsia, The Most Wonderful Secret In The World, Graphite,
Formaldehyde

The Sun beginning to sink below the horizon just as Becca steps up to
the mic. It is one of those magical occasions you hope for both in
music and life, when the disparate elements of Beauty find their
connecting puzzle pieces and embrace, however momentarily. The
crowd swaying along as Becca hops on the comet trails Blish is
expelling and sings them out to the stars. Staying onstage to add some
ethereal oo's - as in the syllable 'oo', not ooze like the slimey
emanations from some interdimensional entity - over the course of the
otherwise instrumental Graphite and contributing adrenalin-fueled
backing vocals to closer Formaldehyde, its most raucous version yet.
Becca commenting afterwards that she is now 'quite an Assette',
which takes a little explaining but the boys eventually get it.

The only thing marring this otherwise stellar performance is the fact
that Max and Brouce had arranged to film the set and when they pick
up the video the following day, once again not a single note of sound
managed to be captured by the magnet of the tape. Max, a strong-
willed sort of fellow, sets about seeing if he can synch the album takes
to the footage but soon gives this up as an impossible feat. His
drumming is always rock solid throughout, but the excitement of
playing live often has him counting the songs in a few bpms faster than
the studio versions. This doesn't stop the band, however, from
watching said video over and over again, mesmerized by themselves.

Despite being such an important number to get right and, as of yet, left out of the set, 38 Nightingale Road gets its debut outing a week later when Hans and Becca - now officially a couple - play their first gig as Nightingale Crescent at Reality Joe's, the local coffee shop opened by one of the former owners of The Reality Café, long since closed down, leaving a very real hole in the caffeinated beverages fabric of the area, as well as in the map of historical Buttery Cake Ass locations.

When Brouce catches wind of Hans and Becca's plans he promptly pays a visit to Reg 'Baton' Button. Who happens to be at the dentist's office at the time. Frantically pacing the waiting room, slurping down something - one presumes a vanilla milkshake - from a large plastic cup, licking his finger to pour salt from a plethora of those little paper packets you get from fast food joints, or, as Brouce had, the inside of a gas station, and dipping said finger right in then scratching his nascent beard with the very same digit, now expressing his concerns over the fate of the band for all the anxious patients to hear, Brouce's hand pointing into his mouth subconsciously reinforcing the discomfort that had brought them there in the first place. 'Shouldn't Hans be putting all his resources into the project he already has instead of starting new ones?' Brouce yammering so fast, Reg sees no opportunity to cut in and suggest that this is hardly the time or the place or that he take a look in the mirror and release the original *Live In Hungaria* as it too is ready to go and has been for some time. The only words Reg can get in edgewise are his response to Brouce's query as to whether Reg himself is going to attend the gig or did he, like Brouce, consider this act 'the willful perambulations of a madman'? Reg replying that he and Blish have had a session scheduled for weeks that same night otherwise he would definitely go support Hans and Becca in their endeavors. Brouce ignoring this, carrying on and on, talking in circles, even after Reg has been called in to see the doctor, spewing out an ever more complicated cost/benefit analysis of heading down to Reality Joe's that night. During which an elderly woman looks up once from her magazine to shrug while the rest of the clientele keep their heads down hoping the angry man will soon leave. Brouce trying to reason with his reluctant audience that 'Hans Floral Anderson is an artistic genius and he wants to encourage him, but in doing so does not want to bring about the end of a group he now regards as his baby, primed as he is to release not one but two of their records any day now.' Such are his last words as the receptionist finally comes out to show him the door. One wonders how Cookie's dad would have handled the situation.

In the end it is Max Beta who convinces Brouce to go. Luckily these two are outside the venue discussing more video plans when Davey Down informs their circle of friends gathered around the table that he too is working on a solo project and is hoping to play Reality Joe's open mic in a few weeks' time.

Walter, having learned his lesson from the Glucose Maman gig, brings a cassette recorder to this one and so catches Nightingale Crescent's first ever performance on tape. I've never seen anyone look as frustratedly excited as Trig when he heard this. Pupils dartin' about the room as if he might spy the legendary owner of Graph City Records there in a corner that has not previously been in the visible spectrum.

But even if by some fluke of nature Walter was to materialize before our very eyes, what are the chances he would have a copy of that particular Nightingale Crescent bootleg with him anywhere on his person? I shouldn't knock it though, stranger things have happened...

Reg and Cookie, both absent, nevertheless received accounts from various sources, all in accord with one another. Becca was a beam of confidence, delivering her lyrics magnificently. Hans more reserved, almost nervous, focusing on his guitar work and harmonizing with Becca's mellifluous melodies. The songs and set as a whole were greeted with enthusiasm and shouts for more. Walter later confiding in Reg that maybe he should've waited and released their Rooftops & Roadways as Graph City's first single. Becca describing her own personal favourites in that letter to Cookie as In Between The Shadows Of The Streetlamps and Blue Balloon, the latter also providing a good description of her handwriting on the page. Each character rounded as if percolating from an invisible bubble machine in the center of the paper. Indeed, such was how she felt singing on stage. It was the penultimate tune, however, the '50s-esque Twin Velvet Hearts, that left a most lasting impression on the crowd.

Blish was still sleeping under the Graph City pinball machine, a way of life he'd become accustomed to. He'd wake up right where he needed to go to work and could relax after hours with thousands of tunes to choose from. By now he's saved up enough money that he decides to buy a used car so Reg won't have to keep coming and picking him up for session work. Per usual, the tan two-door AMC

146

Gremlin he purchases isn't big enough to carry much equipment besides his axe, amp, and pedals, though is again a case of Buttery Cake Ass foreshadowing a major film.

Taking Hans Floral Anderson for a ride to show off his new wheels, the two decide to keep going, much further along the highway, all the way up to pay Brouce Cozzins The Second a visit and find out what is going on with their album. Brouce surprised to see them and quite frankly shocked by their line of questioning. Shaking his head in disbelief as he thought everything was going according to plan, the boys pointing out that there is no plan that they know of. Brouce, scratching his chin and countering that, it now being 6:30 in the evening, any pressing plant he has been talking to would be long closed for the night, inviting them out for milkshakes instead and since they just won't shut up about getting their album released, promising he will make some calls the following day.

Twenty hours later, phoning up Reg 'Baton' Button at his day job with the news that he's sent the tapes off to be mastered at the plant, who will then press the record for them. When Reg finally has the chance to get a word in edgewise, he explains that he doesn't have anything to do with the album anymore, also pointing out that Brouce should really be telling the band this vital information. Brouce is puzzled by all of this, but instead of making any phone calls, feeling the urge to go record shopping, he hops in his Firebird Trans Am and hightails it down to Graph City. Ultimately it is Walter who, after Brouce leaves the shop with another huge stack of vinyl under his arm, picks up the phone and dials each band member in turn. Blish, the last to know, coming back late that night and finding a note from Walter that the pressing plant will ring Brouce within the week about when they can work it into their schedule.

A few days later however, Brouce finds himself, as he sees it, on the receiving end of much pestering from The Man, when he is just trying to make the world a better place by releasing some great music. The record manufacturer informing Brouce Cozzins II that the tape he has sent in is too long for a single album, the maximum recommended playing time for one side being 22 minutes and optimally more like 17. 'Whereas this Buttery Cake Ass', the man's voice sounding incredulous, '...album clocks in at 25:58 on Side A and an even 24 minutes on Side B, both well over the maximum recommended length.'

Brouce's head in his hands, his mind desperately grasping to remember if there is any ice cream in the fridge and vanilla extract in the cupboard, fairly certain there are potato chips on the Lazy Susan. The blender hasn't been washed, he knows, but that can easily be taken care of. After a minute of what sounds to the man on the other end of the line like 'deranged breathing', Brouce asks 'What would happen if we just pressed it anyway?'

The man takes his own deep inhalation, exasperated but used to fielding such queries about this mysterious process from the uninformed. 'Well, it would be much quieter than your normal record,

148

to begin with. And will progressively sound worse and worse the closer the needle gets to the middle, with all the high frequency distortion, especially vocal sibilance and on the cymbals. The last songs on each side would likely sound really bad.'

Brouce pausing in hope. 13th Floorist and 38 Nightingale Road are his least favourites on the record anyway, tunes he has never really understood. He couldn't cut them outright, the band would probably have questions about that, but... And then he picks up on something. 'Likely?' he queries.

'Well, yes,' replies the man. 'Can't say for sure how bad it will be until we press it. We'll send you a test copy of course...'

Brouce breathing a sigh of relief. 'Yes, let's see how that sounds.'

The man replying 'Roger that. We'll send one out to you next Tuesday' and hanging up.

Brouce, still rattled but nowhere near the state of panic he had been in a few minutes ago, replacing the receiver, grabbing his keys and heading straight to the diner. Ordering up three large shakes, the first two of which disappearing before he even realizes where he is. Snatching up the third and signaling for a fourth and fifth to go, Brouce proceeds to the pay phone. Dialing Reg 'Baton' Button repeatedly to no avail. Reg was in a session, Brouce knew, and when he belatedly pauses to consider, surmises that Blish would be there as well. He didn't need any more abuse from 'The Fussy Four' at this point. Still, he should probably seek their counsel. He soon remembers that Max said he would be at Reality Joe's that night, inviting Brouce along. Brouce hadn't planned on going but an hour later he is walking through the door, spotting Max sipping coffee at a table with Davey Down, who for some reason has an acoustic guitar with him. Brouce views Max as someone he can talk to, who is in fact the time keeper of the group and will thus know what to do about this pressing matter. He isn't so sure about Davey Down, but perhaps the bassist will excuse himself and Brouce can get Max's opinion on how to break the news to the rest of band. He greets the Cake Ass rhythm section, puzzled by Davey Down's thanking him for coming and even further confused by Down's pronouncement that he is going to go tune up in the restroom. Shaking his head as Davey Down then walks away carrying said instrument towards said destination, before finally cottoning on. 'He's going solo now too?!'

Max countering with 'He's just playing some of his tunes. I haven't heard 'em yet, but he apparently doesn't think they're Cake Ass material.'

Brouce moving towards the exit mumbling, 'I didn't know. Gimme a ring later, will ya?'

Max putting a calming hand on the label man's shoulder. 'C'mon Brouce, how bad could it be?'

150

And it is these words that dissipate the totality of Brouce's troubles like an opiate cloud descending over his entire body. 'How bad could it be?' Just press the record and it will mostly likely turn out fine, things often do. At all costs, Brouce wants to avoid further hassle from Hans and Blish, and there is now no reason to bring Max into this before anyone has even heard the test pressing.

The relief is obvious on Brouce's five-fifteen-shadowed face, unintentionally conveying to Davey Down that he is enjoying his set. Brouce's mind wandering over his options as Davey's urgent tunes float out into the coffee-scented air of the evening. There was always the possibility of putting out *Live In Hungaria* as a double album, but something about this just doesn't sit right with Brouce. It didn't seem proper for a debut. Presumptuous. And besides, that was coming with the next outing. The never-before-dared live redoing of a band's first album as their second.

There was also the idea of releasing it as a cassette, yes, that would solve everything. But this too is unsatisfactory to Brouce. While he relishes driving around listening to *Live In Hungaria*, and hopes future buyers also copy it onto a blank tape to be able to do the same - requiring, he now realizes, both sides of the tape, unless you get one of those weird 100 minute ones - but Brouce has further reasons for not taking that route. He remembered Paul O. of Hermes Triangle telling him - for he was indeed on friendly terms with the band - that someone once referred to their first album as their 'demo' simply by virtue of having heard it on cassette. Despite it bearing the catalogue number of

ZEUS004, being Ichor Records' fourth release. Brouce knew he would never get over that stigma if he went to all the trouble of releasing a proper record and someone called it a 'demo'.

No, a single album it must be. And it will be fine. By the end of Davey's set, not only has he convinced himself of this but his presence at the performance also helps to quell the other two members of Buttery Cake Ass' fears about the fate of their record. Both too shy to broach the subject with Brouce directly, especially as they were aware that Hans and Blish had already done so, and to little avail, but the fact that Brouce has made the trip down to see Davey play really sets the rhythm section at ease. Hans thinking so too, as he and Becca arrive, holding hands and hair askew, smiling like lovers do, right as Davey begins strumming the intro to his second number. Driving home that evening, all the day's worries seem far from Brouce's mind.

The white label test pressings arrive, three in total, shipped out on Tuesday like the man said, and by now Hans has deluded himself into forgetting all about the possible problems with the audio. Taking the box into his living room and popping one on the stereo, pausing to fix a quick milkshake and grab a bag of hard pretzels. Walking back to drop the needle on Artchery and cranking the volume. Brouce thinking it's sounding great as he sings along with the pinball parts.

In between slurps, nodding his approval to himself that he convinced the band to change the title of the second song to A Real Fridge in Real Life. As the tonearm moves past the recommended 22 minutes per side and The Most Scathingly Brilliant Idea begins winding down, Brouce cocks his eyes and ears at strange snakelike hisses shooting out of the speakers that he does not recall having heard on his cassette, and is greatly relieved when the phone starts ringing as the stylus slides into 13th Floorist, his least favourite song on the album. He spins the volume knob down and heads into the hallway to pick up the receiver.

The call turns out to be from Slice 8, *the* place to play in that neck of the woods, replying to his query about booking the Buttery Cake Ass record release party. A message he had left some months ago when the thrill of it all was still fresh and other exponential plans hadn't yet begun to sprout. The club like the tape, offering him the date of June 28th. Digging the band enough to give them a Thursday night spot, which Brouce snaps up quickly.

And so he resumes his seat on the couch feeling quite pleased about things, sucking up the rest of the shake before remembering the record on the turntable and getting up to flip it over. He knows test pressings are just that, meant to be listened to to check the quality before giving the plant the go-ahead for the full order but even so his mind can't help wandering during side two's opening track, Relics Of Forgotten Futures. His imagination aburst with possibilities now that *Live In Hungaria Live* has been given a recording date. Picturing what the setting will be like that night at Slice 8, rapturous fans in awe of the music that he, Brouce Cozzins The Second, is unleashing upon the world. The first pressing selling out right there and then, minus the ones he would give to Walter for Graph City of course, which wouldn't remain on the shelves there much longer either, word getting out and hungry record company execs bidding the licensing agreements into the stratosphere for *Live In Hungaria Live* and all future releases on Removed Records, keeping him in music, Trans Ams, and milkshakes for years to come. This first snowflake of the avalanche conveniently happening down on 8th Street, mere blocks from Brouce's apartment.

Pausing in his reverie to appreciate the opening strands of his cherished Crumbs, how cool it is to finally have it on vinyl, and is blown away as the needle digs into The Most Wonderful Secret In The World. Becca's joining the band lately for the live renditions really helping it to now stand out for him, as hearing a song in concert will often reinforce its greatness. Feeling how wonderful it is to be the only one in the world to possess this gem, this white label copy of such an incredible album. Full of vim and vigour at Wonderful Secret's closing notes, Brouce lowers the volume on 38 Nightingale Road and walks back to the phone, thereby missing all the sibilance this last track on side two will be spurting as it winds its way closer and closer to the center of the circle.

Eagerly dialing The Man at the pressing plant, Brouce asks if the record can be ready by June 27th, two months away and one day before the big show. The Man, sounding skeptical, telling him to hang on a second as he checks the schedule. Returning after five minutes - this period in between being perhaps the first and only time Buttery Cake Ass has ever been used as hold music, though the record soon ends unnoticed in the background - and giving an affirmative that he could have it ready that day if Brouce will drive out and pick up the boxes. The two then confirming an order for 300 copies, Brouce promising to mail a check within the week. Hanging up the phone feeling very pleased with himself, putting the record back into its blank sleeve and stashing the three test copies away in the fireproof safe in his bedroom closet where he keeps his passport, some stocks his grandfather had given him, and his copy of The Beatles' *Yesterday And Today* with the meat and the doll parts cover. Since he is paying for *Live In Hungaria*, he feels he can do with these test pressings as he pleases, guided more by his subconscious than he will ever realize, tucking these away where no one else will ever find them.

Now that things are in motion, Brouce seems to be picking up messages - signs and symbols - that all will be well. The following day he is overjoyed to receive a postcard from Glucose Maman who are in the middle of their first ever Japanese tour. Mentioning that they had put both songs from the *Formaldehyde Hydro!* 7" on a mix tape for the bus and that their label in Japan - Shattervinyl - love the tunes too. Brouce interpreting this as Shattervinyl would be interested in releasing *Live In Hungaria* and sets about copying the cassette to stuff in an envelope, along with a memo about the possibilities of the label licensing the album from him for a Japanese or even whole Asian territory release. Including also an invitation to the release party on the 28th. Brouce is ecstatic now, almost as much as he had been when that bear mimed what looked like Ringo's arm positions on the *Help!* album cover, and so full of sweetness and light that he feels like spreading more of it. After his trip to the post office, Brouce proceeds to drive down to Graph City, holding the Glucose Maman postcard aloft and beaming a radiant smile as he passes it around for all to read. When everyone had done so, Brouce then drops the news that he has invited Shattervinyl to the show where they can continue talks about licensing the record for the Japanese market. Brouce interrupting Walter's reverie about getting his remaining 70 *Formaldehyde Hydro!*s over there to sell, by asking how many copies of *Live In Hungaria* Walter will take for the shop. For this prospect of a foreign label then was only the tip of the iceberg - if icebergs could be said to be of good news - as Brouce's hairy head has been so full of plans the last 24 hours, he has neglected to tell anyone that he had booked the record release party and that the album will be ready the day before. The band are absolutely thrilled, and in their jubilation, it never occurs to anyone to ask about a test pressing. Nor to Brouce to even mention that any had arrived.

Even with so much else going on concurrently - Blish's session work, Hans and Becca's Nightingale Crescent project, Davey Down's solo tunes, Max Beta embarking on a course in audio-visual technology in the hopes of soon making his own videos, and also everybody starting to read James Joyce's *Ulysses*, which Blish had picked up one evening session waiting around at Reg's for his turn to record, becoming engrossed in it enough to mention the book at practice the next day, intriguing the others, Hans and Becca reading passages aloud to each other on warmer Sunday afternoons in the park... - even with all this, Brouce's multitudinous news sends them into a period of sustained focus on Cake Ass activities. Carrying on the momentum unleashed that day in the shop, the set grows tighter and tighter. 38 Nightingale Road now truly a powerhouse worthy enough to end a show with, and the colour interludes prismatic beyond what they ever dreamed possible. The band even running through *Formaldehyde Hydro!* b-side Gekyll & Seek to prepare for the eventual tour of The Far East that Brouce assures them is coming. And as creativity gives birth to creativity, there are plenty of ideas for new tunes too.

What seems crucial is performing *Live In Hungaria Live* live before they attempt to record it, the key being to find a venue that will let them play for over an hour. Once again Byron Thebes to the rescue by suggesting they host their own show at the abandoned-light-bulb-factory-turned-rehearsal-space, and while they're at it, why didn't Hans take over the room on the other side of the second floor if he is so anxious to get out of his mother's house, especially now having a girlfriend. The DIY craze has been sweeping the nation, as they read about in the zines that found their way onto the Graph City racks. Why shouldn't they put something on themselves? It is highly doubtful that any of their friends in town will make the trip to Slice 8, what with it being over an hour away, except for whoever they convince to help drive the equipment up, and as long as they keep it under the radar of the authorities, a gig in the practice space might even be fun.

Hans nixing Max Beta's suggestion to make a flyer, not wanting the address written down anywhere, and so the event is promoted solely via word of mouth. Walter and Blish passing the info along with their change to any customer purchasing suitably cool records at Graph City's counter. Walter even selling a few more copies of *Formaldehyde Hydro!* as a result to these music enthusiasts always on the lookout for new sounds.

Hans deciding to mark the occasion by moving in that night, making the show a sort of housewarming party as the days too were heating up and getting longer now. Enlisting Blish to help him drive his mattress over, the two bungee cording it to the roof and each holding on through the Gremlin's open windows. The size of Blish's car means leaving a handful of items back at Hans' mother's house to pick up on the morrow. Meanwhile, Byron, Becca, and Max Beta run around town procuring a keg and assorted snacks for the evening's festivities.

A small group of friends arrive early, there being nothing else particularly to do on this Saturday evening. A few now putting down their beers to help Hans carry his stuff up the stairs. Watching strangers approach the door, hesitantly asking if this is the place, the band are once again awash with that curious mixture of excitement and nervousness. Blish and Walter pleased to see everyone who had taken a chance on the *Formaldehyde Hydro!* 7" eventually making their way through the doors.

By 8:45 the place is in full swing, Byron wandering over to the Cake Ass corner with a big smile on his face, suggesting they should do this more often. That DIY is the future, happening all over the States now - New York with Sonic Youth, Hollywood on the Sunset Strip, DC with Dischord, San Antonio, Boston, Cleveland, Detroit...they could even have touring bands play when they're coming through the area. All agreeing that having The Socket, as Byron is proposing calling the place, as a stop on the national indie rock circuit would be pretty awesome.

Buttery Cake Ass taking the stage at 9pm, not wanting to risk a noise violation if it goes too late, projected to end around 10:30 anyway as things stand, with them, ever productive, hoping to blow off steam after finishing what will comprise *Live In Hungaria Live* by trying out some new tunes and maybe a cover or two. The room dimming and Byron turning on the stage lights, all hooked up to the generator, ready to illuminate set and setting as he envisioned, and in his mind just as important as the sounds themselves. The boys strapping on their instruments and launching into Artchery. The abacus now back in play and better than ever. Listening to the band gripe about reproducing the pinball machine sounds on the record and how they'd love to have a real game up on stage when they can afford it, even if Faust had done it ten years before, inspired Byron to help them out again, designing a new abacus that triggers said pinball sounds when struck. Byron making it also able to mimic the balloons popping on Crumbs. And tonight the oh-so-much-more-than-a-counting-device is taking its maiden voyage through pleasant seas. Byron hitting its frame with the spotlight as Blish sweeps his Gibson SG headstock along its beads or Hans flicks them with a flourish of his finger. And in the true spirit of a generous creator, Byron is still, even as they play now, brainstorming ways he can alter the contraption for Max Beta to use as intended. The main problem is still Max's being stuck behind a drum kit that would obscure the audience's view of all things abaci.

The crowd loving what they are witnessing. Moving closer and closer to the make-shift stage, heads nodding in hypnotic appreciation. Walter noting that the new owners of *Formaldehyde Hydro!* do not look disappointed. Very much the opposite, in fact. The applause following Artchery's 12-plus-minutes enthusiastic and somewhat unexpected. Hans and Blish letting chords ring out before the slide into Sepia - the plan, of course, is to blend the songs together - but after a hesitant second or two when the drums stopped, the clapping began, along with affectionate exclamations of 'Yeah!' The band never having experienced anything like this before. As there are those present who had bought *Formaldehyde Hydro!* and as a result then came to see them live, it could be said this is the first time they are playing in front of fans, the realization striking each of them in turn as they then swivel ampwards to obscure their swelling smiles. Max soon kicking in the beat to Sepia, the performance of which many remember as the best thing BCA ever did, now bolstered by visible appreciation, and the thrust carrying into A Real Fridge In Real Life. All ascending towards heights heretofore unglimpsed until the room is plunged into darkness and the stringed instruments rendered virtually silent, Max

Beta drumming on for another few measures amidst the ensuing confusion.

Byron Thebes, being the only one with an inkling of what might be going on, rushing to the wall switch and flicking on the main lights so everyone can see each other's puzzled expressions. Byron checking and announcing what he has suspected, that the generator is kaput. Having acquired the device used from a man keen to get out of town, countless hours of rehearsal have now chosen the most inopportune time to take their toll.

Becca making her way up to Hans, taking his nervously twitching hand in hers and motioning to the expectant crowd, telling him to go grab his acoustic guitar. Whereupon Hans hangs his head and replies it's back at his mother's house. The group attempting to hide but the red of their flustered faces instead providing a beacon for those who want to tell them how great the set was before it got cut off. There seeming to be a sea of these folk blocking departures to any possible exit, and the shame won't disappear no matter how many times Hans and co. hear they should feel otherwise.

Walter, though feeling for the band, senses that they've actually made some new fans. Ones who genuinely want to talk about music with the boys. And as there's still plenty of beer in the keg and snacks on the table it's a while before anyone thinks to leave. Davey Down handling the brunt of the interactions as Blish has snuck off back to Graph City while Hans takes to sheltering in his new room. Byron Thebes bouncing around, excitedly chatting with the partygoers, eager to do more of this now that he's confronted the logistical problems of turning the place into a venue and found they should be easy enough to solve. Purchasing a new generator, from a store this time, should be covered by what they take in at the door over the first couple gigs. Max shocked that people are asking when their next show is and assuring him it can't happen twice. But despite their interlocutors' good intentions, both drummer and bassist feel an even sharper sense of having let everyone down when these strangers declare how much they love *Formaldehyde Hydro!*, the title tune of which was coming up next in the set right after A Real Fridge In Real Life.

By the end of the evening however, Max and Davey, having spoken with Walter, are, if not feeling better about the whole experience, at least presented with proof that this is merely a hiccup. Walter encouraging them that what happened tonight may very well give at least some of the attendees incentive to come see them live again - always leave them wanting more, which, by virtue of not playing anything anyone was familiar with, they did. Blish and Hans' immediate abscondings offer the two guitarists no such perspective, there now appearing to exist a chasm between how all four perceive the event.

Despite the lingering embarrassment, in the course of the following week members of Buttery Cake Ass will run into various attendees of The Damned Blackout, as they have taken to referring to it, the band still baffled by the positive reactions they are receiving and these

162

strangers asking them when they are playing again. The power dynamic within the group seems to switch, at least temporarily, as Max Beta and Davey Down grow more outspoken in order to combat Hans and Blish's sulky reluctance. In the end, there is only one thing for it, to press on. The path of least resistance being a track back to the bowling alley, explaining to new owner Layne 'Big Ears' Arnold their desire to perform for over an hour and why this is necessary. After listening attentively, Arnold agrees, if they'll do it for free and won't require anything from him beyond the space, giving them a Tuesday night in two weeks time at 9pm.

For reasons that can never be entirely clear, they decide to bill this as a secret gig, assuming the alias Bluffing Candy Aardvarks for the occasion - a callback, perhaps challenge, to the earlier adversity faced at the same venue - and set about promoting it mainly through Graph City, as flyers bearing this name won't mean anything to anyone. Indeed this serves to confuse even Brouce Cozzins II, who - having missed The Damned Blackout by virtue of flying to Arizona to catch Van Halen's *1984* tour, something no one could ever fault him for - responds in the negative when asked if he's going to see Bluffing Candy Aardvarks, and remains clueless up until the day after when he runs into Reg 'Baton' Button who fills him in on how it went.

Which was pretty well. Reg informing Brouce that judging by how tight they were, it should be all systems go for the June 28th recording. Brouce phoning up Hans Floral Anderson to make sure that they will still be performing under the Buttery Cake Ass moniker, especially for the record release party, the name having goodwill, or at least Brouce planned on making it so.

Back at the bowling alley, the atmosphere had been expectant. The band naturally anxious, sending Byron and Reg on multiple pre-showtime electricity inspections to eyeball any possible problems that might arise. Not that they saw any, or would necessarily know how to fix them if they did. It did cross both my and Trig's mind that if they had burned down a bowling alley perhaps such notoriety would have propelled them to greater fame, riot shows and cousins thereof bein' all the rage in the history of rock music. But the nerves work their way out into the vibe, Artchery sporting an accentuated angular beginning, the abacus parts now entering the territory of free jazz as balls barreling down lanes collide with pins at odd syncopations to the music. Hans and Blish noticing this around minute six, then gauging their swipes of the beads to strike in time with the spares. Quickly realizing that too much of this is making the music too straight, and thus set about alternating synchronizations and syncopations, Max Beta remaining inscrutable throughout all the havoc.

Again applause, the dancefloor more crowded than you would think for a Tuesday night. Some of the bowlers even stopping to watch every now and again. Sepia charging into A Real Fridge In Real Life. Which, Reg relayed, was rather stilted as all four bandmates braced themselves for what they assumed was inevitable. When the song ends without a hitch, their equipment continuing to function properly, they cast amazed looks at each other throughout connecting piece Butterscotch before charging triumphantly into an unforgettable version of Formaldehyde Hydro, its raucous ending greeted with wild cheers from the appreciative crowd. Momentum pushing them onwards and upwards. The lights flicker during Relics giving all present quite a scare. Carrying on into Crumbs with a collective sigh, the rendition of which Brouce Cozzins would be kicking himself to have missed. Fuchsia exceptionally jubilant, halfway through which Becca begins to glide queenly-processional-like out to her microphone centerstage for a performance of The Most Wonderful Secret In The World that eclipses anyone's love of the group thus far. Afterwards, those who had previously purchased *Formaldehyde Hydro!* at Graph City in the run-up to the gig asking when they can get their hands on this particular tune. The Cake Assers gleefully responding 'June 28th'. But before they come offstage it must be said that the closing 38 Nightingale Road is everything they had hoped it would be, with Byron's light show augmented perfectly by the flashing red of a lane in need of maintenance.

Retiring to the diner once again despite not having been paid and Brouce not being there to foot the bill, the need for celebratory fries surpassing these other considerations. Walter informing the band that he noticed someone, a gentleman who had been present at the short-lived Socket show, bootlegging tonight's gig. A tape player in his hand, standing back by the mixing booth to get the best sound. Trig hangin' his head here, eyes clenched in deep thought, apparently wonderin' how he could ever track down such a person and procure said tape.

The following day Walter is as surprised as anyone to look up and see Layne 'Big Ears' Arnold strolling through Graph City's doors. So pleased is he with the business the bowling alley bar did on a Tuesday night, Layne is keen to give the band another date. Hans phoning 'Big Ears' Arnold back later that evening to accept. And so Buttery Cake Ass plays again two weeks later, an even more triumphant set. Brouce Cozzins declaring as he treats them all to milkshakes and fries at the diner afterwards that they are ready - READY! - and he for one cannot wait for the record release party, pounding the table for emphasis despite having to catch his shake glass from spilling every time he does so.

Byron and Reg kicking back in the diner booth, both feeling pleased with themselves. For tonight they have finally shaped the audio-visual components into something special, only half of which will find its way onto the recording of *Live In Hungaria Live*, the ki-bosh having been put on Max and Brouce's plans for a simultaneous film only yesterday when Brouce, sent into another financial panic after bouncing a check, convinces Max that shooting the concert will put too much of a strain on his attentions, as the drummer will of course want to be involved in all matters of camera set-up, but should really rather focus all his energies on making the music as powerful as possible. But even if it's just the album, who can say how much the light show will influence everything else in the room that evening? Or if Byron's physical proximity to Reg is pushing the soundman to excel past his own personal best? When people call Byron Thebes 'The Fifth, Sixth, or Seventh Buttery Cake Ass' - and yes, some even using that exact phrase - it is not for nothing. And of course the same could be said for Reg 'Baton' Button, using those very words.

Flyers had also been passed out this evening for the record release party, and eagerly received, despite each side knowing that the takers never much leave their hometown let alone would be up for driving over an hour each way to see a gig. The excitement that such a thing is happening is enough to suspend disbelief for the time it takes for a promise to attend to be extended and graciously accepted.

Everyone walking out of the diner feeling on top of the world - Hans hand in hand with Becca, Reg, Blish, and Byron enthusing about the sonic heights reached that evening, Davey, Cynthia, and Angelina pleasantly confused about what's happening, if anything, between the three of them, Max visualizing the feature film his band's sounds will one day soundtrack, and Brouce lingering a moment behind to savour it all, this first step on the road to global domination. Staring down at the flyer he will tomorrow photocopy three hundred times and give to a team of college kids looking for work to paste around the city, paying them in beer and free admission to the show, Brouce feels a fierce sense of satisfaction at the way everything has come together.

This will turn out to be the last gig before the record release extravaganza, as the next day Brouce receives a phone call from Slice 8 management informing him they have a strict policy about no appearances within a 25 miles radius the same month as an event at their location. To keep said date Buttery Cake Ass will have to cancel playing at the warehouse party happening in two days' time that Brouce had set up in order to win over new fans in the area and get as many people down to Slice 8 as possible. The band taking this news in stride. If the last two bowling alley performances are anything to go by, they are on their way...

The morning of June 27th arrives and Blish and Hans are excitedly awaiting sight of Brouce's Trans Am on the horizon, the two Buttery Cake Ass men having taken the day off work to accompany Brouce on the trip to the pressing plant, desiring to be there at the birth of their baby. Even The Man's odd manner when he hands over the six boxes can't put a damper on their enthusiasm. This will be held over another three hours until the squad arrive back at Graph City.

The trio exuberantly barging through the record shop's doors to be met by cheers from Davey, Max, Walter, Becca, and Reg, who had also kept his calendar free these two days, for the release party and, as excited as everyone else, to hear his first foray onto 12" vinyl. As the cardboard box opens and they are each handed a copy of the album, it is a feeling they're sure they will never forget. Gazing upon the 12 X 12 square of the cover with grins nearly as wide, slicing open the cellophane, removing the black disc within... Brouce handing Walter the 20 records he ordered for the shop and Walter taking his own copy and placing it on the turntable, cranking the volume for Artchery to reach out through the speakers and grab them by the throats, rendering the gathered group speechless. Davey Down breaking the silence 12 minutes later as A Real Fridge In Real Life kicks in. 'This is awesome.' All agreeing via nods and smiles. It being a good 18 minutes of bliss before anyone noticing anything that might be considered amiss. Max tuning in to the fact that his cymbals don't sound right, or perhaps the word is 'good'. Not wanting to actually stop the record from spinning, Walter, Blish and Reg hover over the vinyl as it makes its 33 1/3 rotations per minute hoping to catch glimpse of a scratch or specks of dust that might - at a long stretch - explain these aural discrepancies from the recorded version they were used to.

As 13th Floorist begins, Walter lowering the volume so they can concentrate more. Noticing now how quiet it really is. With sibilance even more exaggerated, and strange distortions not attenuated to please. Brouce still in stages of denial, opening up another copy, handing it to Walter. 'Try this one'. All holding their breath until they hear the same again. Brouce quickly flipping the side and turning up Relics Of Forgotten Futures, wiping sweat from his brow before wrinkling it to announce, 'sounds fine'. The others not yet suspecting that Brouce had anything to do with this. Becca sullen in anticipation of her only appearance on the album coinciding with where the sound seemed to deteriorate on side one. Graph City now a hotbed of anxiety. Brouce trying to salvage the situation by bouncing around the shop to Crumbs with a huge smile forced through all the scraggly hair on his face. One that will collapse as he spies the tears in Becca's eyes once her vocal on The Most Wonderful Secret begins. Which in truth is nothing compared to what is coming up on the last track. Reg mercifully yanking the needle from the groove before they can get there. 'What happened, Brouce?'

'What d'ya mean?'

'Why does it sound like this? Didn't you order a test pressing?'

Brouce gulping. 'Yes...it sounded fine...I don't know why this is happening...I'll have to have a word with the pressing plant, they won't get away with this! We've got the record release tomorrow...'

Walter handing Brouce back the twenty copies he had taken for the store. Each member, however, not wanting to part with theirs. For - aside from its defects, the reality of which they can't fully grasp at the moment - this is the first time their music has appeared on 12" vinyl. And oh what music it was, recorded right there in Graph City.

Brouce doing his utmost to keep the others from seeing his full state of panic. 'Don't worry, I'm on it...' and striding faux-confidently from the shop to hop in his car and flee the scene.

Reg, after everything he's been through with Brouce thus far concerning the record, aware of all his myriad proclivities, having caught the name and address of the pressing plant on the box before Brouce's hasty exit, picks up the phone and dials directory assistance. Soon having The Man on the line and getting the whole story. Hanging up calmly and looking Hans in the eye.

'Brouce did get a test pressing. Which sounds identical to this, of course. And he was warned, multiple times, about the record being too long, which is why it sounds so bad. The man was very nice, wished he could help us out. But a double record or cassette are really the only solutions if we don't want to cut any songs...'

'What ones would we cut?' Davey Down, eager for a solution.

'Well, he said we'd need to cut at least four minutes off side one, and two minutes from side two. And more if we want to be able to press it louder. So maybe the last song on each side?'

Becca breathing a sigh of relief. Max offering, 'Could maybe release them as a separate 7"? They do go together thematically...' Hans wrinkling his nose at this, still not seeing any connection between the two tunes. But it was a moot point - *Live In Hungaria* had been conceived and recorded as it was. It simply would not do to perform any surgery on it now.

Hans, silent until this juncture. 'Maybe we should just start copying the original onto blank cassettes, get it out that way...' Turning to Walter, 'Those Cleaners From Venus tapes you've been getting in are great...'

All nod in agreement. If the 12" hadn't been in their hands and spread about the counter looking so cool, self-releasing cassettes would be the very thing.

'We can't have him sell these, can we?'

'I don't know. He didn't seem too concerned about it...'

'The songs have come so far anyway...' Blish begins. The idea lingering and everyone sensing what he is about to propose. But he won't continue with the thought. Yes, having lived with them for so much longer, tested and polished live these many months, the songs are fuller, though now a completely different experience, and the plan had always been to have both. Abandoning *Live In Hungaria* as just some sort of blueprint, a mere demo, for *Live In Hungaria Live* would be completely unacceptable.

'Are we still gonna play the gig?' Hans asks, a legitimate concern.

Max refusing to think otherwise 'Yeah, man. If nothing else, it'll be our first time playing in the city. We'll show them what we got!'

But despite that rallying cry, the evening's final rehearsal is full of dour and defeat.

Three cars meet at the formerly abandoned former light bulb factory the following day at 3pm. The band had taken off work weeks ago in anticipation of this monumental occasion. Now wishing they hadn't. They could use the extra money. But shifts have already been covered and it seems best to stick to the plan. Arrive early for soundcheck, get some dinner, and soak up everything about the whole adventure, despite it having been soured before it even began. The morning and early afternoon, previously imagined as being full of last minute details and preparations are mostly spent in bed, dreading all possible outcomes except for their record magically correcting itself.

No one has been able to get in touch with Brouce. No one is sure what they'd say to him if they did.

Loading up the cars silently. The band going together in Max's Datsun Cherry to keep their sense of solidarity. Hans wishing Becca could join them seeing as she is part of the Cake Ass, part of him, now. Kissing her goodbye, as she will be driving Cynthia and Angelina up along with a good amount of the equipment. Byron Thebes taking the rest, and Walter, in his car.

Becca, despite her own disappointment, leans up to whisper to Hans 'Stay gold, Floralboy' as they part, and over the course of the hour long drive, the excitement of what is happening - a proper show at a proper club, in the big city miles away from home - begins to outweigh the despair of the past 24 hours. Brouce was many things but he sincerely loved their music. Despite his mishandlings, he had actually paid money to get it on record. And they'd heard him enthuse over the countless other groups he loves and grow amazingly animated whilst doing so - bouncing on his heels, voice breaking from the sheer amount of words racing to get out over his tongue and past his lips about each album in his collection, the only thing really calming him down being a long pull off a vanilla milkshake - all of which can't help but endear him to them. He wasn't a bad guy, and he'd set up this awesome gig. There was no reason to sink the ship before they sailed.

Getting lost off the exit when they reach the city - with no sign of Becca or Byron's cars ahead or behind - proves to be nothing an unfolding of the map in the glove compartment can't correct, and so they pull up in front of Slice 8 only ten minutes later than planned. Hopping out of the car to stand below and gaze up at the marquee, confirming what they can't quite believe they'd seen through the windshield - BUTTERY CAKE BAND.

Reg bounding out of the club's doors. 'I know, I know, we're working on it...' Awkward silence for a minute as Buttery Cake Ass scratch their heads and mill about observing the pavement. Blish eventually asking 'Where's Brouce?'

Reg, who has been there a couple hours already setting up the recording equipment, nods 'In there. He's really giving them hell about the name.' Reg, tellin' it to Trig and I, couldn't help but chuckle. That was 1984 after all, the letters in question spelling out what would very much be considered obscene.

174

Soon an older man appears carrying a ladder. 'You Buttery whatever?'

They nod.

'Even if you are talking about a donkey like your crazy manager is claiming, we still can't display that word.' Climbing up and replacing the B-A-N-D with A-C-T, thereby preserving a BCA stronghold.

Hans asking the man once he returns to the concrete, 'Is he in there?' None being particularly keen on running into Brouce Cozzins though all suppose it is inevitable.

'Said he was going out for some fries and a shake, cruise the bars and sell some more tickets. Be back for soundcheck.'

The band looking over at Reg.

'Yeah, I finally got him on the phone at 3 o'clock. Wanted to see if this was still going ahead, and that I'm still getting paid. I can't tell how delusional he is. Seems to think this Japanese label will take care of everything. The album will fit easily onto a compact disc, apparently solving all our problems. CDs are big over there too, where they were invented...'

Everyone squirming uneasily. Sure, this is pretty exciting, futuristic even. But they'd never even seen one of these compact discs yet, let alone knew anyone with a player. Not even Walter, who, although skeptical about the sound quality, is intrigued by the technology.

Becca and Byron's cars pulling up behind them now, each vehicle having been given the same set of directions. Drivers and passengers stepping out on street and sidewalk, pursing lips quizzically up at what they read on the marquee, only to be directed by the man with the ladder to get back in and drive around to the rear doors where they should load in. After doing so, the nine of them returning to find the spots in front of the club taken. Choosing to see this as a good sign, that people are getting there early, they set off to find other parking spaces, planning to meet again in front of Slice 8 before getting some food.

The band are back first and as they are waiting for their cohorts, a couple emerges from the club's front doors as bubbly as a freshly uncorked bottle of champagne. Stylish in all black, she with additional red beret and white scarf, the man calling out, 'Hans?'

Hans whirling around, scrunching up his face. 'Blane?...What are you doing here?'

Blane Blanc, who in homeroom grades 7-12 competed daily with Hans Floral Anderson over who could draw the better KISS logo on their brown paper bag text book covers, turns out to be the first opening act this evening, with his one man project Blancout.

Davey and Max excited to see him now too, Hans introducing Blane to Blish, with Blane then doing the same for the knockout next to him. One Wendy Drops, recently returned from living in Seattle. These two full of life and enthusiasm for everything that is happening, genuinely pleased to see those Blane regards as old friends, that the Cake Ass are playing such a cool show tonight, and that he gets to open for them.

Their acquaintance going way back. By virtue of his favourite KISS song being Rock Bottom, Blane had nominally been in the original line-up of Hans Floral Anderson's The Floorists. Though at the time Hans had him down as playing bass, the sounds of which Blane only ever produced from the lower ends of a keyboard, not exactly what Hans had in mind. But Blane is doing so on stage now, having moved to the city a few years ago and continuing to experiment with synthesizers in his apartment, more widely acceptable after the appearance of MTV than it had been when they were in high school. Blane had even passed a tape on to Walter after Graph City had financed the *Formaldehyde Hydro* 7", though, still smarting from the experience, Walter wasn't looking to release any more music.

Walter and Byron arriving, followed closely by Becca, Cynthia, and Angelina, all surprised and pleased to see Blane again. The group setting out to find somewhere to eat close by. Wendy leading them to the local falafel emporium around the corner, open til 3 AM 365 days of the year, a frequent stop for her and Blane after nights out at Slice 8. The latter often pausing in his catchings up with Walter over their shared love of Cabaret Voltaire to smile at how his girlfriend is captivating the crowd.

Walking en masse, they don't get far before a head-in-the-clouds, mouth-on-a-straw, beard-impossibly-thicker-than-yesterday-to-the-point-where-it-looks-fake Brouce Cozzins II nearly barrels into them, sucking hard on a milkshake, hurrying back to the venue, only realizing who he's run into when he's right upon them. Brouce greeting the band as if nothing is amiss, immediately asking if anyone from Shattervinyl has arrived at the venue yet. Before following it on the next beat with 'Y'all as excited as I am? Tonight's the big night. See ya back there!' and scurrying off scratching his face before he can even be introduced to the newcomers. To whom now, with a deep sigh, Hans takes up the tale of their record label woes and all that is happening with the sound of the album that they were due to be celebrating this evening. Blane and Wendy most sympathetic as the conversation spills over between sips of mango or tamarind juice and mouthfuls of hummus.

Blane, sorry for his old friends' troubles but sensing that no one wants the night to be spoiled, points out, 'Well, it's awesome that Johnny Seizure & The Romans are playing with us. They're huge locally and will draw a crowd.'

The pitas and plates arrive with everyone approving of the choice of restaurant and delighted at how good the meal is, even if pre-show nerves keep the musicians from eating much. Wendy joking that maybe they'll return to grab a midnight snack, as they now make their way back to Slice 8 to soundcheck. During which they get two minutes into Artchery before the lights start flashing and a voice comes through the monitors 'if everything is sounding ok, we're all set on my end, gotta get the next act up here...' Hans shouting back, 'We need to try one more mic.' Becca coming up to run through the first minute of The Most Wonderful Secret before the same voice interrupts with the very same words. The band looking to Reg who, after 30 awkward seconds of final checks on the recording gear with the venue's soundman breathing down everyone's necks, gives the thumbs up.

Buttery Cake Ass are pumped now. Milling around the merch table not quite sure what to say to Brouce with regards to selling the album, still undecided if they're really against the idea. The display looking so cool with both a 12" and 7" side by side. Even if they wanted to broach the subject, Brouce is buzzing all over the venue hanging up handmade signs informing the yet-to-arrive public that it is indeed Buttery Cake *Ass* who are playing this evening, asking every member of staff if the Japanese label have arrived yet or phoned, telegrammed, sent a message in any way, not ruling out international carrier pigeon, and generally making a nuisance of himself.

As Johnny Seizure & The Romans begin to set up, Blane bounds over, enthusing about the three minutes of music he did get to hear of Buttery Cake Ass. Wendy, as if reading his mind, cuts in to tell Hans and Blish that they should have Blancout remix one of their songs, the prospect of which sounds appealing enough to the two Cake Assers.

Casting a glance to see Brouce busy with some masking tape on the far side of the room, Blish picks up a copy of *Live In Hungaria* and hands it to the couple. 'Let us know which tune, and we'll get you the tapes.' Blane and Wendy accepting the 12" appreciatively, genuinely wondering what it sounds like from what the band have told them of its trials and tribulations, then stashing it in one of Blane's equipment cases so they don't have to carry it around all night.

The excitement of being in the city at this legendary venue keeps Cake Ass & co. on the floor to watch the soundchecks of Johnny Seizure & The Romans and, of course, Blancout. Cynthia snapping photos of everything, even the stamp on her hand that gets her in for free. Reg respondin' to Trig's question about seeing these pictures that he has no clue what happened to her, not sure if he ever even spoke to Cynthia much back when she was around.

When doors open at 7:30, Hans, Blish, Davey Down, and Max Beta are watching with awe as people they don't know make their way into the venue. Wendy holding court around the merch table, regaling the group with stories of all the cool bands she had seen in Washington state - The Fastbacks, Bam Bam, Ten Minute Warning, and her personal favourite, Malfunkshun. Hoping they'll come play Slice 8 one day. Such is Wendy's charm that the whole Cake Ass entourage fall a little bit in love with her, causing them to stand much closer to the stage during Blancout's set than they otherwise might have. Byron jumping in to do lights for his old friend, making the performance more visually interesting than just one man standing behind rows of machines would normally be.

Brouce - while half-paying attention to the blips, chirps, gronks, and crunches emanating from Blane's equipment, and digging the pop-infested sea they splash along - is still very much preoccupied with scanning the room for any sign of a representative from Shattervinyl. Trying to play it cool, Brouce's unconscious clawing at his beard every few seconds nevertheless draws any would-be onlooker's attention up to the desperate look in the man's eyes.

Blane leaving the stage to a smattering of applause, in truth more than he is used to, this being his biggest slot so far by far. The 500-capacity venue packed now, eager for the hometown heroes to come on. Some even dressed in Johnny Seizure & The Romans t-shirts with little red-plumed golden gladiator helmets on the breast. The crowd pushing forward as the lights dim again.

Johnny Seizure, good-looking and full of electric swagger, makes his way centerstage, wearing sunglasses and puffing on a cigarette dangling from his lips, unable to take it out of his mouth as his arms are confined in a straightjacket. His backing band evenly divided between the sexes, all attired in togas, though the male guitarist and drummer sport the previously mentioned gold helmets on their heads, while two, it must be said, beautiful girls handle bass and keyboard duties, wearing wigs that have the appearance of the knitted blankets Hans remembers his great-grandmother sitting in her rocking chair crafting. The frontman gives the nod and they power into their first song, over the duration of which, Johnny Seizure escapes from his straightjacket whilst continuing to smoke his cigarette. Despite their new wave aesthetic, The Romans deliver a deeply soulful rock that hits you right in the guts. It's little wonder they are doing so well. Over 45 minutes, Johnny Seizure prowls the stage, whipping the crowd into frenzy after frenzy, relieving himself of a gamut of emotions that transform the room into a sweaty, writhing throng.

Buttery Cake Ass can't help but be caught up in it too. They've not played enough gigs in their career to think in terms of 'tough act to follow', rather they're thrilled to ride this energy The Romans have gifted them. Brouce meanwhile, despite no sign of anyone from any Japanese label or even the college students he had hired to flyer, is also enjoying the proceedings. Dreaming as he gyrates of releasing albums by all three groups playing tonight, having each go multi-platinum, and to think it all started here at this event he had set up. If only anyone would buy the records, something that has yet to occur this evening. At his last count, it even seems someone has stolen one.

Johnny Seizure bids the crowd good night to rapturous cheers while the Cake Ass move to get on stage as quickly as possible and capitalize on the vibe. Although it only takes 20 minutes for The Romans to unload and Buttery Cake Ass to get tuned up and into position, by the time they turn to face out into the venue, instruments in hand and ready to rock, the amount of open space on the dancefloor has greatly, one might say astronomically, increased. Hans can clearly make out Cynthia and Angelina back by the merch stand, who now move awkwardly forward to show their support, joining the smiling, encouraging, Wendy and Blane in the middle of the room. Becca, waiting in the wings, looks out at the rest of the crowd - a handful of stragglers, none of whom anyone else knows, though it would take all of 10 seconds for everyone to introduce themselves and get on a first name basis.

The venue lights dim and a wave of heavy exhaustion overtakes the Cake. Everything they've gone through lately steamrollering over them, though in the course of their spirits flattening an even deeper fury emerges. Blish bashing into the introduction to Artchery, throwing himself about like a thunderstorm of liquid mercury. If this wasn't rock n roll, someone might think to grab Johnny Seizure's straightjacket. If they could catch Blish that is, for all the band seem blurs of light whipping across the stage as A Real Fridge In Real Life and especially Formaldehyde Hydro break new land speed records. The abacus and its pinball machine sounds continuing to be triggered - smacked with flying hands as they rush by - well into other songs that never dreamt of playing host to such metallic parts.

Anyone there that night would tell you that they outdid even The Romans for energy. Pissed off and magnetic, Buttery Cake Ass drew the tiny crowd closer and closer to the stage as they made their way through the songs off *Live In Hungaria* in an epically turbulent chaotic noise. No talking between tunes. Hans is too angry to speak, which in some ways is a blessing in disguise as Brouce had been planning on editing out any banter from *Live In Hungaria Live*, it being assumed

Hans would at least thank people for coming to their record release party. But there is barely anyone there to thank, and the band are too wrapped up in their own exorcism to notice the mesmerized onlookers that do make up the slight but enraptured congregation. 13th Floorist comes alive in a way none had ever expected, frantically seguewaying into Bronze and out the other side with a pulverizing rendition of Relics Of Forgotten Futures. At the end of which, Blish is grinding his face and forehead into the abacus, Reg taking the cue and adding effects in from the mixing board, creating what to all in attendance think might be the complete meltdown of the venue's sound system. The tension too great now and as Crumbs always provided relief with its twist on Relics' melody, it does so here by going way the other way, diving, jabbing, and jousting, a jungle cat too feral to be contained in its cage. Reg wondering if, this being Brouce's favourite song, the group are destroying it on purpose. Only it is far from wrecked, more the sound of coal being crushed into a diamond sped up ad infinitum to a blinding glare of instantaneous bling. The effect on Brouce is devastating. No longer able to hide from the stunt he's pulled, he clasps a copy of *Live In Hungaria* to his chest whilst wringing his hands, the vinyl shattering at first impact. Brouce then grabbing various shards of the plastic and running them along his face as if attempting to shave off the unwieldy beard and his burden of guilt. Walter keeping an eye on the boy as he seems only seconds away from some kind of mania, and perhaps it is Becca's angelic voice on the following song that prevents such an episode. For, as the band are busy tearing themselves apart in a most spectacular fashion, she provides an anchor into the past to remind one and all what is so special about this now wildly off-the-rails unit. There isn't a dry eye in the house even halfway through The Most Wonderful Secret In The World. And if this had been some sort of big Broadway production, Most Wonderful Secret would have been a fitting denouement with a brief scene of final happiness to finish things off as Becca exits stage left to much applause. But emotions are too raw and Graphite's interlude only seizes Secret's grace in its newly-grown fangs. The loveliness of the duet having given new life to Buttery Cake Ass as they now tear through boiling-point-perfect set-closer 38 Nightingale Road. Becca, who had indeed stepped into the shadows after her slot, takes up her spot at the mic again, well-versed in the song, having played it acoustic with Hans plenty of times, to treat all ten audience members to a version no one could've guessed has not been meticulously rehearsed. Brouce overjoyed that this surprise event is being captured and will come out on *Live In Hungaria Live*, far overshadowing the recording on *Live In Hungaria*.

The band screech to the end of their set, dripping with primal passions but not yet completely spent. Every time they look out and see Brouce Cozzins II, that vast anger returning, and now launching into a never-before-performed-live, with Blish anyway, Gekyll & Seek, knocked about at rehearsals when they believed a Japanese tour was imminent and the fans there would of course be calling out for both sides of the 7". Brouce shouting 'YES!', sensing that this will greatly help sales of *Live In Hungaria Live* in the Far East market. Due to the set's now improvised nature, there hadn't been an instrumental interlude before it, but Brouce considers that perhaps one can be made in the studio for continuity's sake. The same going for what follows. For, fires still blazing, Blish flings himself into the opening riff of new song Game Of Cygnets, the title taken from *Ulysses*, and the most fully formed of the latest tunes they have been composing. Hans, Max, and Davey Down happily joining in, with Reg and Byron following suit on sound and lights, figuring out on the fly this angular rocker they've never heard before but are entranced by. Towards the end of which, Blish and Hans lock eyes as divine inspiration descends, both flipping their guitars in their hands to hold them by the necks like baseball bats, and on a nod, together smashing the abacus to pieces. Byron so in tune with the band that he maneuvers the gels and strobe at this new twist to create the effect of thousands of shooting stars exploding over the dancefloor. As the beads fall inaudible onto the ground, Max thrashes about on his kit, the others ramming their axes towards the amps for great washes of feedback, in a makeshift ending for this Game Of Cygnets, a tune that will very literally turn out to be their swan song.

Stunned silence until all realize this this is the end. Hans toys with the idea of speaking to the audience for the first time that night, letting forth an 'Ever get the feeling you've been cheated?', before thinking better of it, unplugging his instrument, and walking off stage to find Becca. Brouce running up to them, ecstatic, 'That was amazing! Incredible! This album is going to be massive.' But the band are depleted, too tired to judge their own performance. Whatever they may have gotten out of the experience remaining intangible as the venue is now eager to move everyone out the exits, bar sales having dried up over an hour ago.

Reg particularly excited, handing them over a cassette that he's recorded via the main multi-track mix. 'That was really something else tonight,' patting Hans on the shoulder and returning to pack up the equipment.

The frazzled four piling back into Max's car. Becca kissing Hans goodbye and telling him she'll see him at home. Cynthia and Angelina hugging Davey Down, leaving him still confused as to what is going on and with whom. All perking up momentarily at their goodbye pecks on the cheek from Wendy who tells them they were 'fantabulous' and that she can't wait for the next time they play. After checking with the club's management one final time that Shattervinyl Records hasn't actually shown up or communicated in any way, Brouce comes outside, ebullient as ever, raving about how great this is all going to be. The band too exhausted to pull back the reins, to even consider that maybe he learned his lesson from *Live In Hungaria*, and that while they are sorting out correcting those mistakes, wiser now, he'll do what is required to release *Live In Hungaria Live* properly. They barely register the strange red markings the streetlamps are flagging up along Brouce's cheeks. Taking their leave of him blabbering away on the sidewalk, making vague promises to Blane Blanc about a record deal.

As Max turns the key in the ignition, Blish asking 'What did you guys think?' All too fatigued to put what they've just been through into words. Hans eventually sighing, reaching in his pocket to hold up the cassette Reg gave him, 'Well, let's find out...'

Sliding the tape into the player to hear a hiss. Hitting eject to flip to side A and rewind. They've merged onto the highway now, a long straight shot home. Although they had played for nearly an hour and ten minutes - the cassette being one of those dreaded 120 minute affairs, not known for their quality - even if they make it back before the recording finishes, they can continue to drive out into the night mesmerized by their masterpiece...

But then still hearing that hiss.

Each staring through their enervated states at the rectangular hole between the volume and radio tuner knobs. Hans cranking the former in the hopes of hearing, well, anything at all.

Big gulps. Hans finally muttering, 'Reg said this came straight from the mixing desk and that he'd tested the set-up at soundcheck. We should be hearing what was recorded.'

After another couple minutes as despair deepens at the realization of yet another album going down the drain, Davey Down hoping against hope that all is not lost. 'Maybe someone bootlegged it?'

'Who?' Hans, Blish, and Max asking in unison, wondering which of the ten attendees might've had the wherewithal to do so.

Davey Down shrugging, knowing they wouldn't be able to release a Walkman recording anyway.

Nothing is said for the remainder of the car ride, though by the time they get out of the vehicle, the band is over. All departing in silence, just like on that cassette. The final word spoken within the Datsun Cherry providing a fitting epitaph for how the world would come to view Buttery Cake Ass.

EPILOGUE - CANDLES IN THE BREEZY ATMOSPHERE

And yay, just like all Shakespeare comedies end with a marriage - despite the tragedy of the band, and of the world not getting to hear its music - so too does our story. Multiple nuptials, in fact. As you like it. But before we arrive at the altar, there is of course much to fill in.

At the end of 1988, completely out of the blue, some might even say a deeper shade of aqua(rium)marine, Hans Floral Anderson received a telephone call from Hans Floral Nightingale, the latter acting as if no time at all had passed. Hans Floral Anderson knowing better than to question this. On the other end of the line, Hans Floral Nightingale immediately begins raving about his latest musical discovery - 'that crazy Fugari band' - and the purpose of his call, indeed his reemergence into the world, is to inform his former associate that the two of them need to make the pilgrimage to Connecticut to see them play the following spring. Hans Floral Nightingale's aunt Petunia lives a little further upstate and the two can stay with her after the show. Hans Floral Anderson is reasonably sure his old friend means Fugazi, whose first EP Hans Floral Anderson had heard the week before and bought immediately. The passion and its three songs beginning with B reminding him of his old band, not that Buttery Cake Ass ever sounded anything like Ian MacKaye ever did. Hans Floral Anderson is naturally curious to catch them live and of course further intrigued by this surprise phone call invitation. So come April 7th, the two ex-custodians of the Floorist faith make the drive, reminding me and Trig of our long journey to New York to meet Cookie. There is much to catch up on along the way, and soon Hans Floral Anderson begins to feel that he might broach the tricky subject of his continuing relationship with Becca. Hans was never sure of the other Hans' true feelings for the woman, especially after his outbursts that night at the band practice that had led to the temporary adoption of Bitter Cashew Advice. Hans noticing the road snacks include no such nut. But Hans and Becca are due to be married that August. The offer of a place to stay at Hans Floral Nightingale's aunt's house greatly helping to cut the cost of a hotel as the couple save for their future life together. Cookie, who would later relay all these details, told us that her place, in Manhattan back then, would have been about equidistant to the club as Aunt Petunia's house but Hans Floral Anderson didn't tell her about the trip until after the fact. A good thing, she considered, as seeing Hans Floral Nightingale again after so many years, and hosting him as an overnight guest no less, was something she'd rather not have dealt with at the time. Becca feeling much the same way but is, as always, supportive, and encourages her fiancé to go, for Hans Floral Nightingale popping back into their lives like this is a major occasion indeed. As Fate would have it, he comes and goes, picking up and dropping off Hans Floral Anderson, without, much to her relief, her ever having to see him.

The show is killer, at Norwalk's now long-departed legendary The Anthrax, with a particularly rousing version of Glue Man. Hans Floral Anderson is familiar with the material as he guessed he might have been, though he isn't actually sure he isn't going to see an act called 'Crazy Fugari' until they get to the club and see the flyer. Still buzzing from the gig, they arrive at Aunt Petunia's house well after midnight to find that her son, Hans' cousin Leif, has only hours ago returned from a clandestine elopement in Copenhagen. That evening being the first time the family meet his new bride, Ethel. The Hanses are put in the guest room next to the newlyweds' quarters and, riled up from the gig and their shared history cascading back to them via the magic of music, the power that had brought them together in the first place, the two talk long into the night. For Hans Floral Anderson has no idea if he'd ever see Hans Floral Nightingale again. All this in a most peculiar setting, as aside from the confounding conjugal circumstances imposed upon the house earlier that day, the décor of the place itself is quite extraordinary. For Aunt Petunia's passion in life, after her son, is penguins. The house is full of penguin posters, penguin paintings, penguin pillows. The guestroom where the Hanses are contains a large bookcase displaying hundreds of penguin figurines of various sizes and in various settings - diving for volleyballs, cheating at pinochle, even performing together in an Arctic polka band, the fiddles stringed with icicles - and, displayed on the chairs and dresser, penguin stuffed animals in a vast array of Nordic sweaters and multicoloured galoshes.

In the far corner of the room a four foot plastic blow-up penguin complete with a shocking pink bowtie stands gazing stoically at the two intruders. Amidst all the discussion of their past and future glories and dreams, and perhaps inspired by the zaniness of their surroundings, the two young men decide it would be quite funny to knock on the newlyweds' door at various points in the very early morning and inquire if they need anything, such as 'a glass of soy milk' and/or 'unburnt toast'. The offers continue - 'You guys alright for sunglasses?', 'Interested in hearing an a cappella rendition of any Captain Beefheart songs?...Your choice, of course...', 'Did you bring any tunics and do they need to be sewn or repaired in any way?' - and many more volleying between them until long past dawn. They never actually venture outside their penguin-infested walls but over a late breakfast it is revealed that their laughter at such possible antics had kept the newlyweds from having a proper night's whatever all the same. The peak of such hilarity coming around 4:30 AM when the Hanses commence laughing themselves senseless at the suggestion of kicking down the door and marching into the newlyweds' room crouched behind the blow-up doll and announcing 'I'm The Marriage Penguin'. Hans Floral Anderson considering the whole evening and this idea in particular a good omen for his own upcoming matrimonial union. Hans Floral Nightingale keeps stumm about it all.

Back home, after what Hans Floral Anderson considers a most excellent adventure, tying up what loose ends he could of his friend disappearing so many years ago without a word - for truth be told, though it was still great to spend time with him, Hans Floral

Nightingale wasn't all that forthcoming about his missing years even now - as he steps out of the latter's car, Hans Floral Anderson invites him to the wedding. To which Hans Floral Nightingale simply nods and drives off.

The big day comes and there has been no further contact between the former bandmates. Blish Billings is to be best man, for despite the fact that the two have not worked together in any creative capacity since that fateful evening at Slice 8, he and Hans have remained close, speaking often even after Blish's departure to Chicago. Hans encouraging all Blish's musical efforts there, of which there are many. In fact, Blish has to take two days off from touring with his then-current and forever mispronounced outfit BB Gum, prime Friday and Saturday spots in fact, to attend the bachelor party and wedding. Davey Down is just back from a German promo tour for his third solo record, *Camel Escalator*. The single Caramel Escalator has been doing quite well in Southern Europe and he will be heading back there the following week. Davey Down isn't the type to miss his friends getting hitched, especially as it will give him the chance to see his muses Cynthia and Angelina again and provide fodder for his next release. Max Beta takes the train in from Kansas City where he is finishing his degree in cinematography. Early bassist Dave Up sends along a platter of fancy assorted pastries as a wedding gift/peace offering.

Although all four members of Buttery Cake Ass are present, and Becca had joined them for all their most spectacular shows, the band think it best not to attempt any sort of reunion. Not that such a thing would even be on the radar to most in attendance. But Hans and Becca, who have their own Nightingale Crescent EP coming out on the same German label as Davey Down, do get up and play a handful of songs at the reception, including a lovely acoustic rendition of Joy Division/New Order's Ceremony. The pair moved to the city in the intervening years, and have recorded a number of homemade cassettes with some real gems on them. These sold out quickly at Graph City and the few mail order catalogues that stocked them. A best-of compilation taken from these tapes was released on vinyl in Spain earlier in the year which led to the EP of all new material.

Now of course Cookie had mentioned some of these projects when we met up with her in Brooklyn and they immediately went to the top of Trig's list. And although she told us that Blane Blanc, as fitting his initials, was also in BB Gum with Blish, skippin' those tour dates as well to attend the wedding along with the divine Wendy, only later did we learn that Blane and Davey Down had released a record together under the name of Down & Out on a small Parisian label. As this has been the story of Buttery Cake Ass, I hope you will understand my relegatin' mention of these later individual endeavors to this epilogue. For the saga of Trig and I's attempts to find these, includin' Reg 'Baton' Button's extremely rare 1989 solo effort *Ace Of Wands*, would take up a whole other book. And of course during these years Trig was to fall in love himself, and time spent amongst the bins and boxes of barely staying afloat record stores understandably dwindled. He was still buying about $500 worth of music a month, doing much to keep those shops going, but the time he had to actually search out new sounds became much more concentrated clock-wise.

Trig met Greta at the local duck pond, walkin' down as he would to gather his thoughts for a few minutes after work before headin' out to a record or book shop. She was leanin' over the railing feedin' the one swan amongst the bunch and Trig, noticin' her red shoes and thinkin' she looked just like an angel, asked if she was an Elvis Costello fan. Greta, lookin' down and laughin', replied 'Kate Bush'. These two words captivated Trig's heart.

After some casual conversation, during which she places half of what remains of her loaf in Trig's hand to feed the avian congregation below, talk turning briefly to the *Mary Poppins* soundtrack, he asks for her number and a pen. Greta swiftly replies, albeit it with an inviting smile, 'If you want to call me, you'll have to remember it'. Repeatin' the seven digits over and over, Trig practically flies back to his car, grabs the marker he keeps in his glove compartment, and scrawls the seemingly magical passcode onto the insert of the Cure's *Wish* cassette, the nearest writing surface to hand, sittin' on his dashboard as he had had a hankerin' to hear Doing The Unstuck that morning. Of course, in line with the record's title, he hopes these numbers will add up to his heart's desire. I am shocked that night when he tells me all this, as normally Trig would never deface any sort of release, such urgency provin' how special this woman was to him right from the get-go. Describin' her to me as 'beautiful, charming, awesome'. I knew that from that moment on our time together would be limited. But I was determined to finish what we had set out to do - find the legendary

Live In Hungaria album.

It seemed I was now mannin' the ship, with Trig spendin' every
moment he wasn't actually with Greta, making her mixtapes. I didn't
dare bring up the fact that the power of these sacred communications
would be greatly enhanced by the addition of a Buttery Cake Ass tune
if only we could find one. For what if Trig were to shrug this off?
Voidin' all we'd worked for these long, long years. No, the thought
was too much to bear. Luckily I noticed that Nightingale Crescent's
rendition of The Most Wonderful Secret In The World as well as a few
gorgeous instrumental tracks from Blish Billings' post-BB Gum
project, Miniature Reptiles, made the track listings of these cassettes.
The flame still burned.

As the year 2000 flips through its calendar pages, with eBay making
albums much easier to obtain and allowin' me to procure almost
everything I ever hoped for except those two Buttery Cake Ass
releases, somewhere in the midst of it all, Trig proposes. I hadn't seen
him in a while, when one Saturday morning he calls me up to head out
to Goose Train that very afternoon. When we had gotten back from
Brooklyn all those years ago we had indeed filled Fred in our how our
quest was going. He was as enthralled as we were by the history,
helpin' us to track down what later releases he could, it takin' months
to even get a lead on Davey Down's first post-BCA outing, the *Melt*
EP, excited that the Japanese pressing also came with the five song

Down To Earth extra live disc. On this particular day, whilst perusin' The Wedding Present section, Trig pulls out their debut record and after nonchalantly readin' its back cover asks me to be best man. Of course I accept, but talk about responsibility. I know I have to step up. It becomes imperative to find *Live In Hungaria* and now I have the added stress of a timeline too. I sense all this immediately and with Trig still at the back of the shop, I make my way up to the counter and, pretendin' to rifle through the 7" New Arrivals section there, explain my predicament all the while to Fred in urgent whispers under my breath. He is most understanding and sympathizes that the legendary album remains unheard by our six collective ears. He's been doin' all he can and will continue to, I'm certain, but for the sake of insurance when I get home I call Cookie again to see if she might be able to provide any clues. In her usual effusive manner, she tells me she's delighted to hear from me, which does wonders to alleviate my anxiety. In fact, she says she's been thinkin' of Trig and I since the previous August but didn't have a way to contact us. Becca and Hans had thrown a huge party in celebration of their ten year wedding anniversary and she thought we might like to hear what everyone was up to. She had been quite surprised to get the invite, not having seen the couple since the wedding, but was overjoyed to connect with the old gang again. Plus one of her fillings had come loose and her father could fix it for her for free. She goes on to say she had mentioned us to Hans, Blish, Davey Down, and Max Beta, and they were all very flattered anyone would go to such lengths to seek out their youthful attempts at making music. They themselves hadn't heard those early recordings in ages. Thrilled as I am to learn that the band now knows of our existence, I also have to stop myself from ponderin' the inherent unfairness of things, with them having copies to actually listen to, heck, even bein' able to call those songs up to sing inside their own heads at the drop of a hat, while Trig and I have sweated over long exhaustive years tryin' to find any information that might lead us to hearin' these records just once, still mystified after so long as to what they could possibly sound like. After a momentary struggle, I'm able to let this go as the tone in Cookie's voice suggests there are further chapters to the story that might intrigue.

Walking in to the banquet hall, the first person she runs into is a clean-shaven Brouce Cozzins II. The two have never met before but Cookie said she recognized him straight away after all she'd been told via letters and phone calls from various band members. He is charming, as she sensed he would be, and one imagines Brouce amplifying this even further in the presence of such a woman. I am to get the full story later when I phone up Reg 'Baton' Button for his renewed help in securin' a copy of *Live In Hungaria*, for despite Cookie's good nature, amidst all the hoopla that evening, no one was too concerned about even dubbing us a copy.

Brouce's face-to-face confrontation with his own dishonesty at the Slice 8 show had led him to nothing short of changing his whole life. The following morning he shaves off his beard and boards a plane to catch the final US dates of Van Halen's *1984* tour, traveling to Indiana, Illinois, Wisconsin, and Texas. Over the next twelve nights, the sheer power of the band, the fact that they could open with something as magnificent as Unchained and still have over an hour and a half left to play, affects him deeply. As Eddie's guitar hits him right in the spiritual solar plexus, Brouce reflects on what he truly wants out of life, what he desires his own set list to become. He knows he must face this honestly, and uphold the truth in his dealings with others. Gone go any inklings that he might one day run for political office or head out to Hollywood. Removed Records would only ever issue the one release of *Live In Hungaria* and we've seen how that went. Nothing is amended in the days following the final show. As the band has broken up, Brouce doesn't see much point in fixing and then promoting the record. Nevertheless, his contrition is heartfelt and he will help all the band members in their post-Cake Ass pursuits - loaning Blish and Blane the money for the first BB Gum demo, acting as Davey Down's agent to secure his German record deal, and financing Max Beta's short film *4:34*. With Hans, he lets him be. Offering any assistance he can, honestly believing Hans is a genius, but not wanting to pressure him in any way. Brouce eventually leaves the music biz game for good, but not before, as great moguls sometimes do, releasing a solo album of his own. Ironically enough, *Salty Shakes* comes out in June 1987 on Shattervinyl Records, preceded by the Ursula Says single, both now selling for astronomical sums. He will go on to become heavily involved with the organic farming movement and sit on the boards of numerous wildlife preservation societies, doing well for himself and the world at large in the process. So delighted is Brouce at the prospect of seeing his old friends again at this anniversary party, he sends along an ice sculpture of three bears miming the semaphore for the letters B, C, and A, along with a delivery of 300 organic vegan vanilla caramel mylkshakes. He is sipping on one of these, with a second on deck in his other hand, when he runs into Cookie, soon pointing out to her the alphabetical ice art. Having no response to this, Cookie catches sight of Byron Thebes and moves herself further into the festivities.

Byron, taken with the whole experience of having been part of the Buttery Cake Ass crew, without any more of that on the horizon, soon after their demise forms a band of his own. The Bulbs never record anything but, in lieu of the Cake Ass, end up supporting Glucose Maman on a few dates when they come back through the area, filling in last minute as their lighting technician, and continuing on in that capacity for the rest of their world tour, burying The Bulbs in the process. It is a post Byron enjoys to this day. The Maman's boys of course remembering how great it had been to play with Buttery Cake Ass and send along their best regards to Hans and Becca on this momentous occasion. Byron's reminiscences of the craziness of the last Scandinavian jaunt are cut short by the arrival of Max Beta, whom Cookie makes a beeline to as soon as he walks through the door, missing out on what happened when Glucose Maman were accidentally hired to play a hospital workers' convention in a small Swedish coastal town on the third night of the tour.

Cookie had been looking forward to running into Max again, being a big fan of the films he has worked on this past decade - *Orange Paperbacks*, *Arbor Night*, and particularly the independent darling of 1992, *Servers*. By depicting the lives of two waiters working across the street from one another in competing early cyber cafés, *Servers* spookily predicted the more asinine traits of the upcoming internet craze. It is charming to look back on now as the film posits such entities would be more like actual restaurants, as dial-up speeds of the time took long enough that one could consume an entire meal or at least a few rounds of drinks during the wait. Hip young crowds gather to 'speak' to each other via the screen, allowing for a tribute to the silent era and its title cards, though the film itself was notable for reviving Technicolor to portray the brightness of this glimpsed future. An era into which however, despite all its advances, confused romantic relationships continued to permeate.

Rather quickly after expressing admiration for his work, Cookie finds herself on the receiving end of Max's grand plans for his pet project, made all the more uncomfortable by Cookie's closeness to the material. For years now, Max has been trying to secure funding for his own version of the Buttery Cake Ass story, or rather the chronicle of the emotional and psychic fall-out he suffered for years after the break-up. Although opening in an idyllic garden with the main character surrounded by leafy greens, his life complete in his love for them, not wishing for anything else, *Charred Remains* becomes a brutal depiction of horror, a mind teetering at the edge of the crisper drawer right before the fridge door closes, the rest of the film largely taking place inside a colossal pinball machine that is filling with milk. Written as a feature, *Charred Remains* would expand on one of his student short films, *Flash*, in which the protagonist is trapped in what might be considered such an arcade game - the budget was too limited to go into that much detail - where wild psychedelic arrows blink on and off pointing to myriad possible exits, every one of which proves false. All the while, in an homage to the opening of *Raiders Of The Lost Ark*, the hero is pursued by a giant metal ball, from which it seems there is no escape. For Max, the ending of that film, when they, spoiler alert, open the ark on the island, perfectly parallels that day in Graph City when Brouce brought the albums back and they heard the disaster for the first time. He often wonders what would happen, legally, if he simply lifted that footage wholesale and stuck it straight into his own film. Max's many design ideas for *Charred Remains* include painting the pursuing spheres - for there are more to be added, just like a real multi-ball game, just like a real band - a deep glossy red to reference both Artchery and the bowling alleys the band had rocked, looming large on the screen and turning into fireballs whenever the game's lights start blinking madly. Most who read the script prematurely point out here that any charring, if this does happen to escalate into a raging inferno, would be nullified by the washing over of the milk. To which Max smiles knowingly and mutters 'Just wait.'

Max is polishing the poetic, animatedly describing the psychoanalytical films within the film that reflect back off the metallic surfaces at the main character, when Blish Billings, whom Cookie had only met for the first time at the wedding, comes up to talk about the video Max is shooting for Blish's new single, Kind Of Rouge, thus allowing Cookie the opportunity to make her escape. Blish is in process of setting up his own label - Bs' Wax - to house his many different recording projects, still going back and forth with his money man as to where the apostrophe should go in the name. While that's been happening though, he's been busy putting the finishing touches on his third collaboration with off-kilter songwriting genius and quintessential British eccentric Nick Newcock as The Knot Crickets, tentatively titled *Knot Knitting*. Their first LP, *BN²B*, was quite a success at student radio stations across Europe, tracks such as Budding Holly and May B Daze allowing Blish to space out in a more pop dimension than he had previously, and their follow-up, *Ntwined*, even got them airplay in the States. Blish is also preparing to reissue his back catalogue on the new label, including such masterpieces as his surf rock album, *Nice Ein*, the *Guitari* full-length from 1991 when he was diving deep into French philosophy and psychoanalysis, fully indulging his Pinhas obsession, *The Emperor's New Threads* EP, and the Dink Tank series of live albums that pay tribute to the music of Nigel Dinks with a full-on guitar orchestra. Throughout all this continuing to be a much sought after session musician.

Davey Down walks in, flying solo this evening. The three chat, but knowing how sensitive Max still is about the band, Davey and Blish don't mention that the last time they saw each other was on a European stage five or six years back. BB Gum finding themselves sharing a bill in Bratislava with The Davey Down Experience, as he was then calling his band, and, roping in Blane, they cover A Real Fridge In Real Life as an encore. The audience, initially baffled by this song they'd never even heard *of* before, were won over by the end.

Cynthia and Angelina both come with their husbands, the same men they had attended Hans & Becca's wedding with, and that had prompted Davey Down to write Long Lonely Time for his next album, *That's Rock N Roll*. The pain of having spent so many years pining for each, of hiring them to provide artwork for his releases and even bringing them into the studio on numerous occasions to sing backing vocals in the faint hope that they'd at last hear his longing, his love, his ardent heart beating true, in the words and melodies he'd composed specifically for their own sirenesque voices, to now have them end up with these fellows still affects him to this day, as heard on Fifth Wheel Finally Punctured from his latest album, *Melt II*. Cynthia is now quite an in-demand photographer, with Angelina, who had formerly been one of her most used models, acting as her agent. Wendy Drops has also posed for Cynthia on many an occasion, designing most of the outfits for these shoots as well, fashion being her trade. She and Blane, now married, are as ebullient as ever, arriving early to the party and staying way past the end, inviting everyone who didn't want to go home after the bar closed to the falafel restaurant down the street from Slice 8, the venue itself long gone. Blane, retired from touring after BB Gum parted ways, continues to release an album every couple of years with Wendy illustrating the covers. Max has been after her to mock up giant boards of his original vision for *Live In Hungaria*, to have a giant metal pinball smash through on film, symbolizing how he felt when his sleeve idea was passed over.

Wendy had designed BB Gum's stagewear as well as Hans and Becca's outfits for their short European tours in the early 90s, playing to enthusiastic crowds throughout Spain, France, Germany, Italy, and

Switzerland, but never making it further East than that. Though the two still release Nightingale Crescent albums, the arrival of the kids has put off any plans for more promotional excursions but they are hoping to take the whole family along when the children become teenagers. The creative force has never left them and they've been writing enough tunes to keep making records for decades.

Becca and Hans are seated at the head table surrounded by their loved ones. Becca's parents have taken little Ariel, now aged five, and the three year-old twins, Jacob and Wilhelm, home after dinner to allow the grown-ups their fun. Toasts are given. The couple to each other, then thanking all those who came along this evening who had been such an important part of their lives. Special mention is made of Walter, no one knowing what he is doing now, but wishing him well wherever he might be.

Continuing on, Hans Floral Anderson stands and walks over to the far corner of the room where right down on the parquet tiles a complete band set-up sits ready to be rocked - drums, bass, six guitars, amps, even a keyboard, plus microphones galore in the hopes that all will join in. Byron picks up the bass, Max hops behind the kit, and the three launch into a version of Bowie's Five Years, the lyric doubled to reflect time married. A half decade ago to the day, Hans had woken his wife up by singing her the original, unaltered, version, measure for measure, and the two carried on throughout breakfast, lunch, and a very romantic dinner serenading each other between peals of blissful laughter. Of which Becca can be seen engaging in now before strolling over to share the mic with Hans as they take the second round of the chorus together, continuing on in their joy.

Soon Blish picks up an extra awaiting guitar and they rock out on Zeppelin's Ten Years Gone and The Verve's A New Decade. Taking things down for a beautiful rendition of The Kinks' Days, Hans singing his heart out to Becca. At the end of which, the song greatly moving for both men also, Byron spots Davey Down lingering nearby and passes the bass off to him.

And so Buttery Cake Ass now find themselves on stage together for the first time in over 15 years. There has been an unspoken understanding that if this should happen no old material would be played, the night was about having fun, letting loose and celebrating. But after the band run through Help!, more Damned than Beatles, and a Third Uncle/Ziggy Stardust medley, more Bauhaus than Bowie & Eno, during a rousing performance of 99 Red Balloons, more 7 Seconds than Nena, Byron Thebes, taking a breather altogether and leaning on a nearby wall, sticks a pin into the oblong sphere floating next to him, green but who's counting, causing a big smile from Max as he then momentarily veers into Crumbs, Blish right there with him as if the two are psychically linked. Brouce picking up on this right away, nearly choking on his mylkshake in sheer delight, already piqued as he was from their playing the tune that had brought him the money to fund Removed Records in the first place. He and Becca catch each other's eyes and begin bursting the balloons around them with great giddy laughs, and soon everyone is popping the decorations in time with the band as they finish out their own beloved tune.

The party atmosphere now up a notch, they blast off into Prince's 1999, followed by Pulp's Disco 2000, a tune dear to the couple's hearts. The only where to go after this of course being Also Sprach Zarathustra, the theme from Kubrick's *2001*, with Blish leading them all off on a jazz-rock psychedelic freak-out, more balloons exploding and partygoers rocking out on whatever instrument or rhythmic surface is at hand, the denouement of which turns out to be most startling.

As if all these evocations of the past contain more potency than anyone realizes, who should now walk through the banquet room's doors but Hans Floral Nightingale. Dressed in a suit of deepest sapphire with a shocking magenta bow tie, an outfit that in a last minute look through one's closet would be met with the words 'this will have to do', and carrying a gift-wrapped square of the same colour scheme. All the various sounds screeching in sections to a halt as each player in turn notices Hans making his way across the room towards their source, Max's drums being the last to die out when he finally spies his old guitarist over the tom-toms. Silence arriving as Hans Floral Nightingale takes his last few steps to present Hans and Becca Floral Anderson with what turns out to be a compact disc labelled *The Marriage Penguin Album*. Its cover looking suspiciously similar to Duran Duran's eponymous 1993 record with a plethora of the Antarctic creatures drawn in, though one imagines the music sounds nothing like the boys from Birmingham of course, or even Arcadia or Power Station... 'Your wedding gift. Sorry it's late,' he mumbles by way of explanation before turning to go.

'Hans, wait!' the stunned Hans Floral Anderson calls after him.

Awkward moment, unsure how to follow this up. Then 'Grab a guitar.'

Another uncomfortable minute or so passes as no one really knows
what to play. Becca taking the reins and belting out the opening lines
to Blue Flower, more Pale Saints than Mazzy Star or Slapp Happy,
beginning with no backing like this, until everyone comes in on the
instrumental chorus. Cookie wasn't sure, but she thought she saw Hans
Floral Nightingale look over at Becca while she was singing the final
line, laying any misgivings in that direction to rest. Anyways things
are moving too quickly to ponder such thoughts, even though no one
has any idea what to do next with the 20 or so bodies now hovering
around the equipment. Some joker fingers the chords to Joy Division's
Decades on the keyboard, met with muffled laughter at its wild
inappropriateness. Or was it, really, considering what they as young
men had set out to do? Inspired by this, Max kicks in the drum beat to
Flowers Of Romance, faster than on record, as is the tone of the
evening. With so many musicians playing, it is impossible to keep to
the minimalism of PiL's music, but this version becomes notable for
its interplay between Blish Billings and Hans Floral Nightingale, the
main guitar geniuses of the two incarnations of Buttery Cake Ass,
never before having been in one another's presence. The context is rife
for brash displays of egotism and power tripping, but amazingly it is
quite the opposite, the two complementing each other exquisitely in

one of the most insane guitar freak-outs Reg 'Baton' Button has ever heard.

Everybody in that corner of the room now in tune with one another. Without any discussion, they shift into Daisy Chainsaw's Pink Flower with Wendy taking lead vocals. At the end of which it seems completely normal to let flow Stephen 'Tin Tin' Duffy's Icing On The Cake, belying their strong pop sensibilities that always lurked beneath the frosting. Even though guitar has been his main instrument these post-Cake Ass years, Davey Down nailing the synth bass part, eschewing the keyboard and playing it on the bass itself. Everyone dancing and laughing, gleefully joining in on the chorus, pointing and nodding and smiling at Hans and Becca right in the middle of it all on the center microphone.

And again as if summoned, the celebratory, yes cinnamon-flavoured, cake is wheeled in while the congregation are bouncing along through the final chorus. Festooned with floral decorations, giving the impression of flamingos against an icy sky, the giant dessert is placed directly in front of Hans and Becca. In the absence of not really knowing what to sing by way of congratulating the happy couple, the partygoers soon find themselves giggling and belting out The Lollipop Guild from *The Wizard Of Oz*, befitting the fairy tale-ness of it all, growing faster and faster with the musicians playing whatever they feel like, whatever is moving them at the moment, the closest anyone's ever gotten to the fabled Ramones free jazz sound. At the end of which, Hans and Becca, barely able to stand from the exultant joy surrounding them, are holding each other up to blow out the candles before kissing the kiss of all the best pop songs. Opening his eyes afterwards with his arm still around his gal, Hans looking around to see so many lifelong friends, those he and Becca had been through so much with - Blish, Cookie, Max, Brouce, Reg, Byron, Davey Down, Blane, Wendy, Cynthia, and Angelina beaming back at him. All except one Hans Floral Nightingale, now nowhere within view. Casting his gaze to the distance, Hans Floral Anderson sees the parallelogram of light implying one half of the banquet room's open double doors fading and, with a soft unheard click, shut. He senses his friend moving away on the other side, heading back down his own peculiar brick road, and knows it must be so. After a moment he looks down at the cd in his hand. If Max were to make a more mainstream film of their saga, this zoom in on the various penguins in full wedding regalia would make a fitting final scene.

Yes, Reg had been there too, and confirms it was quite the shindig when I phone for his help with Trig's wedding gift. I was nervous, Reg being such a busy man and all, cranking out albums that I continue to love. But as his name was actually on *Live In Hungaria*, and Cookie's was not, I reckoned the odds were with him. He doesn't seem all that surprised to hear from me, but perhaps it is simply his relaxed manner blowing off steam after a particularly heavy session with Particularly Savvy Hessian and thus is inclined to talk. He tells me all about Hans & Becca's party, mentioning the guitarist who came in at the end and blew everybody's minds. He'd like to work with him, he mentions off-handedly, maybe getting this guy and Blish in the studio for a collaboration. I get the impression Reg doesn't realize how much work such a feat would entail, even just to track Hans Floral Nightingale down. Reg moving quickly on, telling me how great it was to connect with Blish again, the two having lost touch in recent years due to the diversity of the projects they are involved in, both geographically and stylistically. But they had chatted about making another record together soon, Reg maybe even becoming a house engineer for Blish's new label.

Has Reg heard *The Marriage Penguin* album?, I asked. No, he left the next day and hasn't been in contact with Hans or Becca since, except for a brief email exchange about mixing the new Nightingale Crescent record.

The first lull in the conversation comes about ten minutes in and I feel it is time to get to the purpose of my call. I begin by explaining how Trig has been my best friend forever and rehashed the details of our quest that we had already told him years ago. Sensing Reg might be losing interest, I come to the crux of the matter - Trig's upcoming wedding and how there can be no other gift from me than a copy of *Live In Hungaria*. Reg exhales deeply. He's sorry but he doesn't even own one himself anymore, having ceremoniously burned his in effort to banish a plague of recurring bad sound whilst making Test Inn's *Out With The Old* LP, a ritual that must've been successful judging by his later achievements. He has no idea what happened to the original master tapes or any of the cassette dubs from it, and the fate of those extra 290 records that Brouce had pressed is anybody's guess. Reg doesn't have Brouce's number anymore, though he was greatly relieved to see the changes in the man at the anniversary party.

In desperation I ask him about the fabled *Live At Bootylicious* cassette. Reg chuckles. 'Actually yeah. I do possess the 'true source', as they call it. I could run you a copy of that. Would be perfect for your friend's wedding night, as they say.'

I hang up the phone overjoyed. Trig and I would finally get to hear - though I guess 'hear' isn't the correct word as the tape is completely devoid of sound - but experience Buttery Cake Ass, perhaps in their most distilled form.

The cassette arrives in the mail a week later. I immediately go out and buy a fireproof safe, stashing both in my closet à la Brouce Cozzins II. Despite such precautions, every day leading up to Trig's walk down the aisle is filled with anxiety. I dare not listen to the tape myself. What if it snaps? Or leads me on to the carnal heights rumored by some to be its *raison d'être*, sending me on a spree that sees me miss the wedding entirely and not want to part with the cassette at any cost? No, instead I focus my will on every little detail for the presentation of such a gift to go perfectly. It is vital that I give Trig and Greta the artifact myself, of course, to be in their presence when they open it, obviously before their first night together as husband and wife but after the ceremony. Once *Bootylicious* is in his hands, I know Trig won't be able to hold out more than an hour or two before popping it into a tape player. I buy an inflatable penguin, and two backups just in case, blowing one up and hiding it out of view at the reception hall. Of the standbys, I keep one in my car and the other taped to my back. Sure, it is unbelievably uncomfortable and bulky, but better this than miss out on the chance of a lifetime. When the time comes, the original penguin works just fine - it has not been kidnapped or punctured - and seconds before my best man speech I steal away only to reappear again crossing the dancefloor crouched behind the plastic beast and shouting 'I'm The Marriage Penguin' as I push it towards the happy couple. The penguin carries a silver platter with *Live At Bootylicious* sitting on top. I daren't even have gift wrapped it. Trig nearly faints when he opens the cassette case and takes out Reg's short note of congratulations that also serves to verify the authenticity of the recording. Greta, who has heard the legend of *Bootylicious* countless times, gives me a big hug and I can tell she understands my gesture. The relief I feel when I am finally able to unburden myself of that extra four foot penguin strapped to my back, folded of course but still, is akin to being drunk, and the gentleman I ask to rip the masking tape off only to watch a penguin head unfurl from a mass of black plastic on the floor indeed quickly races to the bar for a drink to recover. Trig and Greta are long gone by now, absconding to their awaiting upstairs suite that I have arranged to have a state of the art stereo system brought into. The hotel warns me about noise ordinances but I assure them that the tape they'll be listening to is completely blank. It is perhaps my greatest gift to them that I patiently wait the week until they are back from their honeymoon to hear *Live At Bootylicious* myself. And oh what a night that was! One that, much like the recording itself, can't possibly be reproduced via mere words.

And so all's well that ends well, as ol' Willy Shakes would say. I haven't told Trig about Cookie's latest revelation of *The Marriage Penguin* album. Why torture the man, especially now that he's embarked on his life of wedded bliss? There is only the one copy in existence and I wouldn't want him pestering Cookie or dragging Greta off on some new insane scheme, depriving her too of many a night's sleep. They'll be experiencing enough of that soon when the kids come, only talk for now but the couple confiding in me one evening that if they're twin boys, the names Hans & Hans are the obvious contenders. Yes, Greta is perfect for Trig. Even designing a special room in their house for his tens of thousands of records. And I think she wants nothing more for him than to increase that collection by a very special one. So the quest for *Live In Hungaria* continues. Dear reader, if you have any leads...

DISCOGRAPHY

BUTTERY CAKE ASS

Formaldehyde Hydro! 7"
(Graph City Records) 1982
Formaldehyde Hydro/Gekyll & Seek

Live At Bootylicious
(unofficial bootleg, no track listing) 1983

Live In Hungaria
(Removed Records) June 1984

Side One: Artchery
A Real Fridge In Real Life
The Most Scathingly Brilliant Idea
13th Florist
Side Two: Relics Of Forgotten Futures
Crumbs
The Most Wonderful Secret In The World
38 Nightingale Road

BLISH BILLINGS

String Theory

(Magnetic Head Records) January 1986

(B's Wax reissue) February 2000

Side One:	Hot Wired
	Series Of Suspensions (S.O.S.)
	Elisabeth Shue
Side Two:	Maid Marian's Net
	Been Frankly Electric
	Forgetful Fingers

Nice Ein

(Octoflash Recordings) April 1987

(B's Wax reissue) February 2000

Side One:	Beach Fuzz
	Foamy Daze
	Tide To The Mast
	Silver Waves
	Elk Storm
Side Two:	Aqueduct Tape
	Hanging Zen
	Blish Boogie
	Devocean Now For The Future
	Rings Around Lemuria

Quarter Roi

(Magnetic Head Records) October 1987

(B's Wax reissue) February 2000

Side One:	String King
	Game Of Cygnets
	Eclairs In F#
	25 To 1
Side Two:	Material Monarch
	Pockets
	Coined Kin Ear

Groaning Pastures [dedicated to Snakefinger]

(Lithograph Records) April 1988

(B's Wax reissue) September 2000

Side One:	The Cows Have Not Left
	Groaning Pastures
	Quickly Mowed
	Olympic Fencing
Side Two:	Stargrazing
	Edward's Hidden Sheep
	Optimal Scarecrow Positioning (If I Only Had A Chart)
	Sally Forth Through The Fields

Guitari

(Le Label Londrette) July 1991

(B's Wax reissue) September 2000

Side One: Winsome Deleuze Sum

Potent Félixir

Towards A Minor Key

Side Two: String Theory

Wry Zone

Le Tempo Moderne

Persephone's Lips

(Collect Call Recordings) April 1994

(B's Wax reissue) September 2000

Side One: Purse Of Pomegranates

Orpheus Next Door

Ichor Tap

Side Two: Fluid Candy

When You Go Away

Super Cedars

Whisp

Curious Accounts

(Collect Call Recordings) July 1997

(B's Wax reissue) November 2000

Side One:	Unbalanced Sheets To The Wind
	All Earsay
	Taxonomies Of Impossible Organisms
	Presents IV
Side Two:	Silence Invoice
	Buffalo Tails

EPs

The Emperor's New Threads EP

(Octoflash Recordings) April 1990

(B's Wax reissue) May 2001

Side One:	Apparent Apparel
	Swift Flattery
	Scenic Lace
Side Two:	Ray Meant to Say...
	Mayhemming Away

7" Singles:

Glimmers Come & Go b/w Railroad Shadows
(First Days Records) September 1985

Cleaning Up The Daybreak b/w Penny Of A Star
(First Days Records) July 1986

A Cruel Word b/w Mot Cruel
(Le Thirsty Records) June 1987

Acetyleaning b/w Legerdemain
(Slightgeist Records) January 1988

Bogus Corners b/w High Strung Harp
(Fans Of Todd Records) July 1992

Whispers Overhead b/w Costly Current Fixations
(Collect Call Recordings) January 1998

Kind Of Rouge b/w Witches Woo
(Orbit Discs) November 1999

Full Tilt b/w Excerpt of Charred Remains Theme
(B's Wax) June 2001
[with Max Beta on drums, pinball, and electronic abacus]

MINIATURE REPTILES

Starfishing

(Small Scale Records) September 1994

(B's Wax reissue) October 2002

Side A: Cast To The Night Skies

            Space Is The Plaice

            Spare Rods

            Catch 23

            Night Boat To Chiron

Side B: Luna Allure

            Shooting Stars In A Barrel

            Five-Sided Secrets

            Diamonds In The Lucid Sky

            Cast To The Night Seas

Karma Klub

(Small Scale Records) October 1995

(B's Wax reissue) October 2002

Side A: Krokodile Dub

            Merging Mambas #9

            Tortoise Bisque

            Cottonmouth Strikes Again

            Iguana Dance With Somebody

Side B: Kimono Dragon

             Alligator Tears

             Python Eileen

             Born In The MEDUSA

             Newt Sensation

Missile Thrust

(Small Scale Records) December 1997

(B's Wax reissue) October 2002

Side A: Blast Often

             Raketemensch

             Red Glare

             Aeneas

             Master The Winds

Side B: Shockwave Goodbye

             Katje Looking

             Songbirds Of Fire

             Dial Mavis

Lizard Mixtures

(Small Scale Records) August 1998

(B's Wax reissue) October 2002

Side One: Cosmopolitan Vinyl

             A Capital Idea

             Wild Wolves

             Uncle Oswald's Stirring Tales

             Brooding Bats

Side Two: One Drop Of Crocodile

Duck Receipt (Soft Beaks)

Memory & Desire

Lasertilia

Even On The Tides

THE KNOT CRICKETS (Blish Billings & Nick Newcock)

BN²B

(Royal Duck Recordings) March 1993

Side One: Budding Holly

May B Daze

Bat An I

Gemini Critters

When, Up On A Star, You Wish

Side Two: Margaret & Susan Go Boating

Periodic Table Settings

Places To Stay Along The Interstellar Autobahns

Ntwined

(Pitch 22 Records) March 1995

Side One: Turquoise Hair

     Wrapped Around Your Little Nose

     Chirp Chirp Slurp Slurp

     Maudlin Allison

     B Raid

Side Two: Six Of The Juiciest

     Obtuse Trickery

     N Gauge

     Conscience Guidebook

     Baskets Afoot

Knot Knitting

(Cin Cin Music) January 2000

Side One: Stitchuation

     Porcupining

     Andy Frog

     Tangler's Rest

     Hey Stax

Side Two: Peel To King

     Fiddlesticks

     Treble Soft

     Not Now, Brown Brow

     Sew Alive

DINK TANK (Blish Billings' guitar orchestra tribute to Nigel Dinks)

Tray Full Of Dinks (Live At Brooklit, Brooklyn, April 24, 1993)

(ReDinkUlous Recordings) September 1993

(B's Wax reissue) April 2000

Side One:	On The Rocks
	Swish Licks
Side Two:	Malaise Maze
	C'est Yeah
Side Three:	Farrah
	Fictional Iceboxing
Side Four:	Trolleyed
	Dink Up

Dinks Cabinet (Live At Calligraphy House, Berlin, October 20, 1993)

(ReDinkUlous Recordings) June 1994

(B's Wax reissue) April 2002

Side One:	Miss Missive
	Hot Voodoo/Hot Tap
Side Two:	Dinks Donks, Which Is Dead?
	Morning Rafters
Side Three:	Vampyro
	Hands Of Steel
Side Four:	Gettin' It On
	Ghostface Thriller

Tradinktional Arrangements (Live At Joan Dark's, New Orleans, July 14, 1995)

(ReDinkUlous Recordings) May 1996

(B's Wax reissue) May 2002

Side One:	Dinky Steps
	Take The B Train
	Jacket Required
Side Two:	Summertime
	Dinks On The House
Side Three:	Early Aspirations
	Blue Nigel
Side Four:	Midnight Triangle
	So Long, Helmut's Strudel

BB GUM

Everybody Move! This Is A Stick Up

(Bazooka Records) September 1988

Side One:	Burst Bubbles
	Forte Knocks
	Juicy Feet
	Triple Pronged
	Once Around The Sun

Side Two: Owl Pops

                Peanut Butter Slip

                Daylight Dancin'

                Heist Heist Baby

                Both Barrels

Ah, Choose

(Goat Parade Records) May 1991

[released in Japan and Australia as *Sophomore Biting*

(Shattervinyl/Reverse Spin Records) June 1991]

Side One: The Big League

                Glued To Your Shoes

                Privatize

                Ears Off

                B's Sneeze

Side Two: Up The Scenery

                Tish Tish

                Frances' Garland

                Wriggling Her Nose

Back In Style

(B's Wax) March 2001

Side One: Let's Rock

                Analogue Lady

                Backyard Pussycat

                Running Over Hot Coals

                High Street Velvet Blues

Side Two: Tongue Ties

Under My Nails

Low Heroes

Glastonbury Groove

Always In The Air

DAVEY DOWN

Melt EP

(Beat Haven Records) January 1985

Side One: Puddle Of Love

Look What You've Done

Side Two: Liquid Hi-Fi

Japanese Fruit

Cauldrone

Lock EP

(Beat Haven Records) July 1985

Side One: (Looking Through The) Keyhole To Your Heart

Sore Lips

Daughter Of The Wise Wolves

Side Two: Sheepish Seagulls

& Spiel

Melt + Down To Earth live EP

(Shattervinyl) February 1986

Down To Earth

Side One: Puddle Of Love

              New Year's Kisses

              Seven Beauties

Side Two: (Looking Through The) Keyhole To Your Heart

              I'm Down (Beatles cover)

Count EP

(Beat Haven Records) March 1986

Side One: 10 To 1

              Pulp

              New Year's Kisses

Side Two: Ferdinand Graf

              Abacus Dust

Tumble

(Beat Haven Records) September 1986

Side One: Overload

              Taurus Moon

              Acrobats In The Belfry

              Four Sheets

Side Two: Seven Beauties

Adore Mat

Shaken & Stirred

Nevermind November

All A Blur

Seven Beauties b/w The Eighth Stranger (7" single) July 1986

All A Blur b/w Leisure Adverts (7" single) November 1986

Upsand

(Discos Pequeños Cuadrados) July 1987

Side One: Cups & Clowns

Elevator To The Stars

Flexible Pentacles

Plain Jane's Speaking In Flags

Side Two: Words Are Swords

Sea Of Saws

Blonde Wand

Game Of Cygnets

Rabbit Up

Cups & Clowns b/w Jugular (7" single) July 1987

Plain Jane's Speaking In Flags b/w Semafive Shadows (7" single)

January 1988

Camel Escalator

(Discos Pequeños Cuadrados) July 1989

Side One: Caramel Escalator

              Airy Dramas

              Kiss Your Teeth

              Easy Rider

              Your Piercing Stares

Side Two: Deserted At The Top

              Only Bouncing

              Over The Sands Of Time

              Mirror Age

Caramel Escalator b/w Toffee Z Rider (7" single) July 1989

Caramel Escalator b/w Toffee Z Rider and Vertically Red (12" Maxi Single) July 1989

Kiss Your Teeth b/w Only Bouncing Over The Sands Of Time (No Forecast remix edit) (7" single) November 1989

Kiss Your Teeth b/w Only Bouncing Over The Sands Of Time (No Forecast remix) (12" Maxi Single) November 1989

Break EP

(Goat Parade Records) March 1990

Side One: Your Autumn

              Puzzled & In Pieces

Side Two: Lapse Co.

              Om Exit

              Sway's Point

That's Rock N Roll

(Goat Parade Records) February 1991

Side One: That Stroll

              Long Lonely Time

              Poking Pencils

              Page Of Her Diary

              Lovers & Fighters

Side Two: Firm Hands

              Up The Garden Path

              PBalloon

              Petulatown

              Bond Flicks

Firm Hands b/w Ja, Besides Dortmund 1984 (7" single) January 1991

Firm Hands b/w Ja, Besides Dortmund 1984 and Palpable Plot Points
(12" Maxi Single) January 1991

Page Of Her Diary b/w Bohemian Bonhomie (7" single) April 1991

Page Of Her Diary b/w Bohemian Bonhomie and So-So (12" Maxi
Single) April 1991

In Through The Outstares

(Goat Parade Records) June 1992

Side One: Enter Sleepy Jean

              Ring Contest

              Blink '92

              Magical Clear Skies

Side Two: Vitreous Echoes

              Caps Off To Fisheye Lenny

              All Exits

              Code A

Enter Sleepy Jean b/w Barrel Of Bluebirds (7" single) May 1992

Magical Clear Skies b/w Warrant Men (7" single) August 1992

All Along The Tower House

[as **THE DAVEY DOWN EXPERIENCE**]

(Low Sails Records) June 1993

Side One: Electric Love I Need

              Hot Spring Burn

              Star-Spangled Manor

              In A Sense

              Tiny Flowers

Side Two: Tyger Tyger

              Loch Ness Bolero

              Catching Mary Spin

              Turquoise Shields

              Euphoric Ribbons

Electric Love I Need b/w Clearwell Castle Traffic (7" single) May 1993

Tyger Tyger b/w On The Prowl (7" single) August 1993

Tiny Flowers b/w Sting Like A Beat (7" single) October 1993

Motels Of The Metaphysical

(Psychic Goat Records) May 1995

Side One:	Check In
	Livin' & Lovin'
	Pretty Vacancy
	Astral Body Talk
	No Nickels, Double Dimes
Side Two:	Boxcars
	Stealin' Taowels
	Egyptian Cotton
	The Pool
	Check Out

Pretty Vacancy b/w Out To Brunch (7" single) April 1995

Boxcars b/w Nicky's Number (7" single) July 1995

By The Seaside

(Psychic Goat Records) April 1996

Sea Side:	Naval Bass
	Ever More Sandy
	Laughing In The Rain
	Arcs Around The Sun (Pisces Intersection)
De Side:	Western Shore
	Washed Away
	Good Tidings Bad Tidings
	Omoo
	The Crawl

Western Shore b/w Fair Of Hair, Port Off Course (7" single) March 1996

Ever More Sandy b/w Conventional Holidays (7" single) July 1996

Sun Beat

(Psychic Goat Records) June 1998

Side One: Golden Fleece (for Elise)

                      Little Darlin'

                      It

                      Brother Ray, Sister Moon

                      Parasolangebra

Side Two: Missed Hopportunities

                      Heliopoly

                      DDT For One

                      Prodigalactic

                      Any Tomorrow

Little Darlin' b/w Long Cold Slippers (7" single) May 1998

Prodigalactic b/w Innocently Drifting Through Another Life In Exile (7" single) October 1998

Prodigalactic b/w Battle Royale (Prodigalactic Synthetic Siblings Remix) (12" Maxi Single) October 1998

Melt II

(Psychic Goat Records) November 1999

Side One: Fifth Wheel Finally Punctured

Popsicle

3 Of Hearts

Angel Synth

Silver Shoes For Ruby

Side Two: Ice Queens (We All Scream)

Fondly Overdue

Puddle Of Red

Thrown Towels

Strange Idols On The Moon

Popsicle b/w Summer Heat (7" single) August 1999

Ice Queens b/w Winter Treat (7" single) December 1999

Down Under (Live In Sydney, Australia)

(Reverse Spin Records) May 2001

Side One: Fifth Wheel Finally Punctured

(Looking Through The) Keyhole To Your Heart

Seven Beauties

Popsicle

Ferdinand Graf

Side Two: Vitreous Echoes

Western Shore

Lemons & Tangerines

Livin' & Lovin'

Your Autumn

Side Three: Long Lonely Time

Plain Jane's Speaking In Flags

New Year's Kisses

Ever More Sandy/Wide Open Road (The Triffids cover)

Puddle Of Love

Side Four: Dave The Stripper (The Birthday Party cover)

Bow Down (The Go-Betweens cover)

Disco Down (Kylie Minogue cover)

Go Down (AC/DC cover)

Ciao

(Psychic Goat Records) September 2002

Side One: A Drip Of Honey

Taste Of Grandeur

Lemons & Tangerines

Custer's Last Slice Of Pie

Side Two: Dot Hog

Fortune Cookie

Blue Swayed Cobbler

Just Desserts

Creamy Cake Collapse

Dot Hog b/w Roar Shack (7" single) August 2002

A Drip Of Honey b/w Bye Ciao Auf Wiedersehen (7" single) January 2003

DOWN & OUT (Davey Down & Blane Blanc)

Bordeaux & Brighton

(Le Label Londrette) May 1994

Down Side: Downtro

Marseille & Manchester

Lunar Lions

Nice New Castles

Lilypadding

Out Side: On The Tiles

Dr. Dijon

The Road To Wigan Casino

Coming Down For Air

Outro

HANS FLORAL NIGHTINGALE

The Marriage Penguin Album (self-released, no track listing) August 1999

MAX BETA
Charred Remains Original Soundtrack (unreleased)

NIGHTINGALE CRESCENT

Roundabout Midnight
(self-released on Tidy Moon Records) July 1986

Side One:	Cygnets & Signals
	Twin Velvet Hearts
	Blue Balloon
	In Between The Shadows Of The Streetlamps
	Mysterious Stars
Side Two:	Rooftops & Roadways
	Orchid Gloves
	The Most Wonderful Secret In The World
	11:52
	Chimes Of Goodbye

Her Lemon Streets

(self-released on Tidy Moon Records) March 1987

Side One:	Petal Path
	Game Of Cygnets
	Her Lemon Streets
	Midnight Tea Parties
	Aburst Ablush
Side Two:	Sad Lotus
	Lunaticklish
	Sour Apple
	Peach Shoes
	Pumpkin Path

Radio Dust

(self-released on Tidy Moon Records) October 1987

Side One:	Sugarstuck Pouts
	Down The Dial
	Blue Prince
	The 12th Of Tomorrow
	Ancestral Rust
Side Two:	After The Teacups
	As Evenings Fall
	Trance Missionary
	Ashen Books
	Delicate Sips

Mainlining Candy Hearts

(self-released on Tidy Moon Records) February 1988

Side One: Echoland

              Sugarpopkiss

              Cupid, Take A Bow

              Love Spike Blood

              Lips Like Honey

Side Two: Sugarcubism

              Tracks In The Snow

              Wait For It

              Tungsten Green

              Message In Vain

Fashion Oracles

(self-released on Tidy Moon Records) August 1988

Side One: Chivalry Boulevard

              Elegant Venus

              Latest Face

              Haloes Under Hats

              Pursuit Of Swords

              Lingering Rays

Side Two: Heart On Sleeve

              Peach À La Mode

              Dancing Chic 2 Chic

              Medium Sighs

              Delphinium Boutonniere

              Poise Annoys

Wonderful Secrets

(Discos Pequeños Cuadrados) May 1989

Side One:	The Most Wonderful Secret In The World
	Twin Velvet Hearts
	Sugarpopkiss
	Her Lemon Streets
	Elegant Venus
	Echoland
Side Two:	Orchid Gloves
	Lips Like Honey
	Delicate Sips
	Sugarstuck Pouts
	Sour Apple
	Delphinium Boutonniere

Modern-Girl Eyes

(Discos Pequeños Cuadrados) January 1990

Side One:	Modern-Girl Eyes
	Sylvia Silence
	Last Two Windowpanes
Side Two:	Dial M For Modern
	Flutterby Kisses
	Her Sugar Cane

Seascape With Figures

(Owl Time Records) June 1992

Side One: Seashell Singthings

Sand Of Gold

Coastal Secrets

Ampersandcastle

Royal Waters

Side Two: Swayed Beside

Figuremarine

Seahorsefeathers

At The Café De La Plage

Princess Ruby

Flyaway Road

(Owl Time Records) September 1994

Side One: Two Lips & Chimneys

Sigillographic Societies

Via Volante

Cloud City

A Dress Unknown (Nigel Dinks cover)

Side Two: Landing Sites For Soaring Eyes

Pavement To Be

Atmospheric Alleyways

Plain Jane At Five O'Clock

North Star Goodnights

Honey Tortoiseshell

(Owl Time Records) May 1998

Side One: Sapphire House

Twisbies Near The Lake

Perhaps Hand

Under The Archways

Miss Olive Ridley

Side Two: Cities Of Calligraphy

Calicozy

Fancy Cover

Steady Ribbons

Creatures Of The Night Seas

BLANCOUT (Blane Blanc)

Modern Mountaineering

(Serene Window Records) July 1985

K1:   Electronic Summit

            Saw Tooth Avalanche

            MT Headed

            Mallory Keaton

            Ice Picnic

K2:   The Uxbridge Road

            Enough Rope

            Jane's Recreational Pastimes

            Strange Arrangements

            Up Above The World

Jungfrau

(Serene Window Records) April 1996

K1:   Modern-Girl Eyes

            Hymns To Leia

            All Her Lines

            Cantonese Bern

            Mother Nature's Daughter

K2:   Young Harts/Young Frowns

            Calcite Maiden

            A Laughable Party

            Sky High Priestess

            Slowly Melting

Paired Peeks

(Serene Window Records) September 1998

K1:   A Matter Of Cream Horns

            First Teardrops

            Cracked Toes At 2600 Feet

            Hoodwinked

            Piz Gloria

K2:   Hillary Mole

            Great Northern Hawk Owl

            Apples On Deck

            Outer Car Paths

            Bells Of The Andes

REG 'BATON' BUTTON

Ace Of Wands

(Magnetic Head Records) June 1989

Wand A: Wanderlust

            Hot Rod

            Will Waves Away

            Resceptre

            Optimystic

Wand B: Speak Softly And

            Love Button

            Torch

            Cloud Club

            Stick With Me, Kid

RECORDED BY REG 'BATON' BUTTON, SELECTED DISCOGRAPHY

Albums

Car Berators - *Munch Kin*
(Camera Flage Records) December 1984
> [featuring Blish Billings on Rudimentary Rembrandts and Express Lane Yourself]

Chuck Fudge - *Spoonerprisms*
(Duck City Records) February 1985
> [featuring Blish Billings on Howler Bat, Tiered Whales, and Urbane Row]

Dentist Tennis - *Ballbreaker*
(Sudden Pony Records) May 1985

State Mottos - *Pointless Heroics*
(Duck City Records) September 1985
> [featuring Blish Billings on Flowers & Such and Highway Japes]

Disaster Routes - *À La Cartography*
(Quadratic Paws Records) October 1985
> [featuring Blish Billings on Maple Syrupt and Menuphoria]

Angry Boating Devices - *Rift Raft*

(Deep Seated Recordings) November 1985

    [featuring Blish Billings on Bad Scramble]

Tragic Magellan - *Floating In Circles*

(Plural Hats Records) January 1986

All Fun & Games - *Overly Dramatic Tactics & Toes*

(Toronto Gardens Records) May 1986

    [featuring Blish Billings on X'd Out]

The Mollusk Men - *Boisterous Behavior*

(Deep Seated Recordings) June 1986

Man Vs. Snake - *Snake Verse Chorus*

(Quadratic Paws Records) September 1986

Conjury Duty - *Well Hung*

(Plural Hats Records) October 1986

Honey Trapezoid - *The Shape Of Things To Come*

(Aspect Wheelie Records) January 1987

Superb Photos Of Lions - *Far-Out Scene*

(Like A Label) April 1987

    [featuring Blish Billings on Maneframe and Age Of Hearts]

Clown Damage - *Dig That Cat, He's Really Gone*
(Former Tents Records) June 1987

Beige Snow - *Wack Frost*
(Camera Flage Records) November 1987

Urchin Up - *Tips From The Ocean Floor*
(Good Reef Records) January 1988

Glucose Maman - *Steady Steed, Now*
(Schneeball Records) September 1990

The Mollusk Men - *Snail Mail*
(Deep Seated Recordings) October 1990

Dentist Tennis - *Occult Racket*
(Sudden Pony Records) November 1990
      [Blish Billings credited as 'slice guitar' on all tracks]

Arachnoprobia - *Eight-Legged Mishearing*
(Octoflash Recordings) May 1991

Deflocked Priests - *Pet Seminary*
(Ostrich Hostage Records) September 1991

Glucose Maman - *Flying Panda O-ttack*
(Schneeball Records) April 1992

Whirlpools Of Despair - *Magellan Infestation*
(Deep Seated Recordings) September 1992

Method Forest - *The Timbre Of Silence*
(Four Thirtyish Records) March 1993
      [Blish Billings credited with 'atmospherics']

Glisten Eleven - *County Fair*
(Camera Flage Records) July 1993

CoEd Serpentine Undertaking - *Hiss N Hearse*
(Many Towels Records) September 1993

The Mollusk Men - *Muscle Beach*
(Deep Seated Recordings) November 1993

D Sector - *Bringing A Frog To A Knife Fight*
(Plural Hats Records) February 1994
      [featuring Blish Billings on Twist In, Shout]

Artist Portraits - *Finnegans Pillow Talk*
(Camera Flage Records) April 1994
      [featuring Blish Billings on Lazy Gentlemen and Crumpled
      Sheets]

Hammermaid - *Aquatic Architecture*
(Good Reef Records) September 1994

Gnome Plumage [featuring Rip Chislesworthington of Clown Damage] - *No Known Plumage* (Mage Da Clown Records) January 1995

No Trick Ponies - *Troubled Troughs*
(Former Tents Records) March 1995

Milquetoast - *Milk & Toast*
(Soppy Salute Records) June 1995

Teflon & Off - *Fickle Friars*
(Tucking Tusks Records) December 1995

Horse Tranquilizers Make Tranquil Horses - *Hit Me Up*
(Sudden Pony Records) June 1996

Vest - *Vest II*
(Worn Out Grooves) August 1996

Harlequinine - *Malarial Medicine Cabinet (Laughing All The Way)*
(Doctoreador Records) January 1997

The Boats - *Dockin'*
(Don Scott Recordings) May 1997

Gnome Plumage - *You & What Spectrum?*
(Plural Hats Records) October 1998

Wry Otto - *They Say I'm A Riot*
(Like A Label) April 1999

Apothecary Nation - *Bottle Royale*
(And Beyond Records) June 2000

Particularly Savvy Hessian - *Smarty Pants*
(Plural Hats Records) July 2001

7" Singles
* featuring Blish Billings on guitar

The Courtesandals - Fetishes Afoot b/w Tripping Balls*
(self-released) 1984

Toad Truck - Can't Catch A Brake b/w Poison Wheels, Lover's Eyes*
(self-released) 1985

Unhip Hoorays - What's All This Shouting? b/w Yeah, Ray
(Questionable Beams Records) 1985

Promenods - Not Waving, Nodding b/w Heavy Heads*
(Bored Walk Records) 1985

Incremental Breakdown - Slow Ride b/w Baby Steps*
(Bored Walk Records) 1985

Scarf Weather - Necking Time b/w Ascottage*
(Lynx Rink Records) 1985

Dr. Cool - Hip Operation b/w Pelvictrola
(Socketball Recordings) January 1986

Irish Birdwatching - Danny Angel b/w Frosty Blue
(Toronto Gardens Records) May 1986

All Fun & Games - Losing On Ice b/w Line Driver's Dead
(Toronto Gardens Records) July 1986

Jupiteriyaki - The Sauceman Always Rings Twice b/w Gas Giant
(Glazed Orbit Records) May 1987

Heinkel Schneinkel - There Is A Pig...(Floating In My Passageway)
b/w All Folks
(Glazed Orbit Records) June 1987

Clown Damage - Mime Pony b/w Mime Little Pony, Mime!
(Former Tents Records) April 1988

The Cut Slack - Slice Of Line b/w Overworked Smoke Stacks
(To The 9s Records) March 1991

Grammatical Sabbatical - Awash, With: Colin b/w ','
(Fiction Earring Records) May 1992

Synchronous Cities - Doublin All The Time b/w Police State*
(Young Stingray Records) October 1993

Narcissist Kiss - I Think I'm Alone Now b/w Kant Resist
(Solipstick Records) January 1994

Metric Hat Trick - Sense Meter b/w 3 Cent Meter
(Toronto Gardens Records) May 1994

Delinquaint - Old Time Faults b/w Late Motifs
(Overdude Records) July 1996

Ponce The Horse - Pincer Neighs b/w Imploring Explorers
(Former Tents Records) June 1998

Blasé For Artist - Drawing Bored b/w Stuck Figures
(Alpha Bed Records) March 1999

EPs

Hairs Of The Cold War - *Close Shave For The Hotheads*
(Way Out Wills Records) September 1985

Meanwhile Coyotes - *Severe Timing Catastrophes*
(Plural Hats Records) July 1986

Insipid Sips - *Sipping Nonetheless*

(Obstinate T Recordings) March 1988

      [featuring Blish Billings on Exsaucerize and Lift Drops]

Clown Damage - *Cool Rollin'*

(Former Tents Records) September 1988

Long Halloween - *Capricandycorn*

(Auld Fang Sign Records) November 1988

Jacob's Latter Days - *Corn On The Twilight Rungs*

(Lime Climb Records) August 1990

Clown Damage - *Frown Management*

(Former Tents Records) April 1992

The Loud Sounds - *Sounding Loud*

(Overdude Records) March 1993

Vest - *Five Eastern Standard Time*

(Worn Out Grooves) February 1995

Hammermaid - *Pink Nails & Pigtails*

(Good Reef Records) May 1996

Forecastor Oil - *Greasing The Wheel Of Fortune*

(Psychic Beaver Records) June 1997

Mime Candy - *Chewed Out*
(Auld Fang Sign Records) March 1998

Weatherware - *Icy London, Icy France*
(Chill Sniper Records) September 1999

BROUCE COZZINS II

Ursula Says b/w Semaphore Bears No Resemblance 7"
(Shattervinyl Records) May 1987

Salty Shakes
(Shattervinyl Records) June 1987

Side A: Salty Shake Quake
             Boys In The Yard
             Ursula Says
             Don't Ask Me Where I Am
             Real Big Dipper
Side B: Kelis Says
             Vanilla Halo
             (There Is No I In) Ass Stance!
             Removal Man
             Grizz

NIGEL DINKS SELECTED DISCOGRAPHY

Studio Albums:

On The Dink
(Starry Day Sounds) July 1966

Side One:	Gettin' It On
	'66 DPM
	Cliff Notes
Side Two:	Edge Boy
	Fresh Hold

Dink It Over
(Starry Day Sounds) April 1967

Side One:	Full Speed Ahead (In The Name Of Love)
	Sketches Of Stains
Side Two:	Venus Infers
	Ponderosa
	D Deuce

Invisible Dink
(Starry Day Sounds) February 1968

Side One:	Dinky Steps
	Midnight Triangle
Side Two:	So Long, Helmut's Strudel
	Miss Missive

In A Pensive Mood

(Starry Day Sounds) January 1970

Side One:	Red Notes In Pink Ink
	Composed
	Wilfully Forlorn
Side Two:	Feather Frolics
	Felt Fountain

Hermetical Hitchhikers

(Sudaphone Records) August 1972

Side One:	Bang A Gong Of Sixpence
	Take The D Train
	Caravaggio
Side Two:	Outdoor Minor
	Copper Gnu
	Spare Tire, Strike Gold

Five Finger Viscount

(Sudaphone Records) May 1975

Side One:	Early Aspirations
	Hands Of Steel
Side Two:	Noblesse Oh Nige
	Frond V
	Abacouscous (Hand To Mouth)

Only Nigels Have Wings

(Sudaphone Records) March 1979

Side One:	Blue Nigel
	Pilot Light
Side Two:	Hot Voodoo
	Bald Bleach
	That Touch Of Dinks

Slam Dink

(Fisker/Buntley Records Ltd.) February 1981

Side One:	Half Courtin'
	Swish Licks
	En Guard
Side Two:	Dr. D
	Nightshade Net

The End Is Ni

(Torte Churn Records) May 1984

Side One:	Sour Cherry
	Fictional Iceboxing
	Moist Moist Moist
	Broken Elevator Buttons
Side Two:	Appetite For Reconstruction
	Swept Away
	Hoist Hoist Hoist (The Petard Song)
	A Dress Unknown

Live Albums:

Everything But The Kitchener Dinks (Live In Ontario 1967)

(Starry Day Sounds) October 1967

Side One:	Farrah
	Hot Tap
Side Two:	Sync Pâté
	Maple Leaves
	Life's Sun (Pertly Flying)

Nigel At The Gates Of Evening (Live in Floyd, New York 1968)

(Starry Day Sounds) November 1968

Side One:	Who Reset The Controls On This Bike?
	Bright Faced Moon
Side Two:	Nigel Of The Morning
	Summertime

BooDinkspest (Live In Budapest Halloween 1969)

(Starry Day Sounds) December 1969

Side One:	Dinks Donks, Which Is Dead?
	Ghostface Thriller
Side Two:	Cemetery Sweets
	Vampyro

Drinks With Dinks (Live In Vienna 1971)

(Sudaphone Records) October 1971

Side One: Razzmajazz

Dinks On The House

Side Two: Trolleyed (Dinks, Dinks, Dinks)

Malaise Maze

Side Three: Make Mine Dinks

On The Rocks

Side Four: Dink Up

Morning Rafters

40 Dinks (Live in Sleepy Hollow, NY, 1974)

(Starry Day Sounds) September 1974

Side One: Midnight Triangle

The Night Has Only One I

Pillow Talk

Side Two: Blank Etiquette

Trojan Hoarse Crane

Skating Dink (Live at Olympiahalle, Innsbruck, Austria 1977)

(Sudaphone Records) June 1977

Side One: Zambonin'

Triple Axels In A Row

Side Two: On The Rocks

Close Shave

Dinky Steps

Tuff As Nails (Live In Tufnell Park, London 1981)

(Fisker/Buntley Records Ltd.) May 1981

Side One:	C'est Yeah
	Backbone Xylophone
	Front Gardening
Side Two:	Odd C's
	Dinky Derek
	D'Assist

Dinks '82

(Fisker/Buntley Records Ltd.) August 1982

Side One:	Jacket Required
	Strate Flush
	Triple Lindy
Side Two:	Ecstatic Plans
	Eye D
	...And You'll Miss It

Dinks-Related Highlights:

Fitzgregory & Falloway - *ff*

(Sidearm Records) April 1973

Side One:	Dim Sum
	Forever Free
	Double Up
Side Two:	Real F'ing LOUD
	Fun Fun (Fun)
	fFade Out (Psych)

Alan Wilforn - *Done IV*

(Sidearm Records) November 1974

Side One:	@ Fledermaus
	Wing And Amiss
Side Two:	Fire On The Wing
	Empty Edifice

Liner Notes

This book is dedicated to my best friend growing up, Brian Ewing. Who, when we were 15, asked the clerk at Cutler's Records & Tapes in New Haven, CT if they had anything by the band Buttery Cake Ass. The clerk looked a bit puzzled, but then asked if there was any particular album we were looking for. Though I was still in shock from Bri's genius utterance, I immediately replied '*Live In Hungaria*'. At which point the man behind the counter looked even more confused and asked if we meant *Live in Hungary*. Bri and I shook our heads no, deeply serious, informing him that it was definitely *Live In Hungaria*. That feeling of utter joy, as the clerk walked away to go check, has always stuck with me. Laughing with such wild abandon that everything else fell away except the sense that what was happening was truly wonderful. And ever since, this is the state I strive for whenever I do comedy.

There are a few others I would like to mention as inspirations for this text.

Despite having grown up in adjacent towns in Connecticut, Vic Sekelsky and I did not actually meet until the beginning of our sophomore years at Boston University, and quickly began to embark upon epic record shopping extravaganzas that even we realized bordered on the absurd. Vic and I shared a love of Dinosaur Jr. and, just before winter break, I mentioned how J Mascis had played on Gumball's *Wisconsin Hayride* EP, and that I loved their version of The Damned's New Rose. It soon became very clear that Vic needed this record posthaste ('buy it yesterday', as our friend Sean once told my sister regarding Hüsker Dü's *Zen Arcade*) and my copy was back in Connecticut. Over several long hours, Vic and I hit every record store in the Greater Boston Area, and back in the 90s there really were some stellar shops there. All this when we really should have been studying for finals, as we had spent the semester blowing off schoolwork to go to shows and, yes, more record stores. These were only the first months of our acquaintance. There would be many more such overinvolved excursions to come.

The truly one-of-a-kind Jim Psarras gave me the names of Blish, Brouce, Nigel Dinks, and Dinks' band and record labels. With Jim and Christian DiMenna, as our band Inbetween, I went through some of what takes place in *The Ballad Of Buttery Cake Ass*, not so much in detail but in spirit. We made some great music together, a colossal sound blending punk and space rock, though when it came time to record or play shows, most everything came out sounding like Misfits and Ramones. We love those bands dearly, but the pressure to impose some form on the music we were creating to then replicate it live obscured our more improvisational natures, and I feel we never truly captured our essence.

The names Walter and Fred come from the great Brass City Records of Waterbury, CT. Walter was Brass' kindly owner who watched my friends and I grow up through Iron Maiden, Britpop, and beyond. He introduced me to so much great music, and it was at Brass City that I finally found one of my own Holy Grails - P.i.L.'s *Commercial Zone* - in the back of a lower shelf one fine schoolday afternoon in 1993. I was, and still am, gutted by Walter's death in 2015. I hope he knew what a huge influence his shop and suggestions were on my life. Inspiring me to get out there and form my own bands, and have ridiculous adventures on par with lots of what went on in this book. A bespectacled, cardigan-wearing gentleman named Fred worked at Brass City between 1992 and 1994 and introduced us to the likes of Sarah Records, Prince Far I, and Snakefinger, to name but a few. I never knew what happened to him after that, but wherever you are, Fred, thank you.

The record shops of 1990s Connecticut were fantastic, and I can't leave out mention of Damon and Phoenix Records, Chris Razz and Secret Sounds, and Malcolm & co. at Trash American Style in Danbury. Malcolm convinced me to purchase Dave Roback's *Rainy Day* LP (for only $8!), and I'll never forget the day I was buying the double disc *The Best Of Nick Cave & The Bad Seeds* and Razz told me I also needed the double disc of Saint Etienne's just-released *Good Humor*. Both of these events were life-changing. Two of many such occurrences. And of course Murray and the short-lived Rhymes Records, up a wooden stairway a few doors down from Cutler's in New Haven, who ordered me the Australian AC/DC boxset for $90 in the summer of 1990, allowing us to hear those great Aussie-only DC releases. The record shop in my hometown was called Graf Wadman, and Jim and I used to ride our bikes down there seemingly every day. You'll note the names. My thanks goes out to all of them.

And, last but not least, to my Aunt Marcia, who always encouraged my writing and many other things, embellished here as Aunt Petunia, and whose own penguin collection led to some very similar post-Fugazi show hilarity, which is another of my favorite memories.

CPSIA information can be obtained
at www.ICGtesting.com
Printed in the USA
JSHW042053161122
33257JS00003B/5